THE
PACHINKO
PARLOUR

Also by Elisa Shua Dusapin

Winter in Sokcho
Vladivostok Circus

THE PACHINKO PARLOUR

**Translated by
Aneesa Abbas Higgins**

ELISA SHUA DUSAPIN

This edition first published in Great Britain in 2022 by
Daunt Books Originals
83 Marylebone High Street
London W1U 4QW

2

© Editions Zoé, 2018
Published by arrangement with Agence litteraire Astier-Pécher
All rights reserved

Originally published in French as *Les Billes du Pachinko*

English translation copyright © 2022 Aneesa Abbas Higgins
With the support of the Swiss Arts Council Pro Helvetia

A CIP catalogue record for this title is available from the British Library.

ISBN 978-1-914198-16-8

Typeset by Marsha Swan

Printed and bound by TJ Books Ltd

www.dauntbookspublishing.co.uk

THE
PACHINKO
PARLOUR

I STEP OUT of the train and plunge into the narrow passageways of Shinagawa Station. Limescale on the walls, plasma screens flashing toothpaste ads, a woman with a gleaming smile. A tide of people rushing by. Outside, workmen are dismantling a building site. A platform overhangs a garden, cherry trees, enclosures where salarymen gather to smoke, puffing jerkily on their cigarettes, stubbing them out on rocks that look like the stones that horses lick for salt.

I follow Madame Ogawa's directions. Take the walkway that leads to the residential complex, building number 4488, buzz the answerphone to let her know I've arrived, take the lift up to the top floor.

The door opens directly into the apartment.

Madame Ogawa is dressed in a tailored jacket, sweatpants and socks. The heat is stifling. She looks older than I'd expected. Perhaps it's because she's so thin. She's sent her daughter, Mieko, on an errand to the shops. She'll show me round while we wait.

A long corridor with rooms on either side, perfectly symmetrical. She shows me the bathroom first. Flesh-toned plastic. So tiny I can barely stand. The bedroom opposite is just as small: built-in wardrobe, brown carpet. A bed with an immaculately ironed bedspread, a second one thrown across it, unironed, piled with a jumble of skirts and T-shirts. A stale tobacco smell hangs in the air.

'This used to be a hotel,' Madame Ogawa says apologetically. 'We're on the smoking floor here. We moved in when the hotel went bankrupt. My husband's a bullet train engineer. He was working on the expansion of Shinagawa Station for the Shinkansen trains. The whole area's being redeveloped. This'll be a hotel again soon, they're supposed to start work later this month. We're the only ones living here.'

She's standing in the doorway, looking at me, her hand on the doorknob. I turn away, feeling uncomfortable in the intimacy of this cramped room with its bare light bulb. I can't see any windows.

At the far end of the corridor, an open-plan living room with kitchen-diner. The stove takes up most of the room, along with the bookshelves. Beyond the picture window, a haze of pollution blurs the contours of the metropolis below.

I follow Madame Ogawa back towards the entrance.

'Mieko's room is downstairs,' she says, indicating a door half-hidden by a coat rack. The door opens onto a concrete staircase. 'Be careful,' she says. 'The light switch is at the bottom of the stairs.'

Her voice echoes slightly, as if in a cave. I feel my way down until the concrete gives way to a springier surface underfoot. The humidity rises. A neon light flickers on to reveal an open pit surrounded by a walkway with a waist-high glass barrier. The floor of the pit slopes gently down to a drainage hole. In one corner sits a single bed.

Madame Ogawa places her hands on the guard rail.

'The swimming pool. It's never been used, even when the hotel was open. Mould. It's clean now, since we had it drained. Mieko sleeps here, for the time being.'

I lean over the barrier to get a better look. Arranged around the bed, a desk and a chest of drawers, a yoga mat and a hoop reflected to infinity in mirrors on either side of the pool. Plastic blocks are arranged at the foot of the

steps leading down into the pool. I can't help thinking of the arcade game Tetris, with the geometrical shapes that drop down and have to be arranged in space.

'Do you like yoga?' Madame Ogawa asks.

I tell her I don't know, I've never tried it. She nods her head slowly.

We go back upstairs. A little girl is waiting for us in the kitchen. Bobbed hair, shorts and a yellow T-shirt. She's sweating, her fringe sticks to her forehead as she bows to greet me.

'I bought salmon,' she says to her mother, holding up a package of ready-made lasagne.

It's only ten in the morning, but Mieko starts setting the table while her mother shucks oysters and puts the lasagne in the microwave. It comes out steaming and she serves large portions to Mieko and me, a smaller one for herself.

She's taken off her jacket. Her T-shirt clings to her ribs, the points of her nipples. A vein bulges along her arm from shoulder to wrist. Desiccated, I think to myself, like everything else about her. The lasagne sheets slither off her chopsticks into the pink béchamel sauce. She

fishes them out again deftly. From time to time I bite into something that feels solid, the salmon probably. Mieko finishes eating and leans back in her chair, her mouth opening and closing like a fish.

Madame Ogawa dabs at her lips with her napkin, folds it back up.

'If you could take her out once in a while too . . .'

'Of course.'

'I was thinking . . . Perhaps you could go and play first?'

'Okay.'

I'm not sure I've understood what she means by 'play'. In Japanese, 'play' can be used for all sorts of things, from children's games to evenings out with work colleagues. In Korean too. I've no idea what children like to do. I'm in my late twenties, I'm not used to being around ten-year-olds. I'm beginning to wish I hadn't answered that ad. 'Native French speaker wanted in Tokyo to tutor ten-year-old during summer holidays.' I'd seen the ad in Geneva, on Tokyo's Sophia University website. Madame Ogawa was a French teacher herself, she'd be busy preparing for the next school year. She didn't want her daughter spending too much time on her own. I'd been planning to spend the month of August in Tokyo with

my grandparents, before travelling to Korea with them at the beginning of September. I was concerned I might have too much time on my hands. I accepted Madame Ogawa's offer and we agreed that I'd meet up with Mieko now and then during my stay.

Madame Ogawa cleans her plate and glances over at mine.

'You don't like it. Have some oysters.'

'No, no, it's good,' I say, forcing down a mouthful of lasagne.

She clears away the lasagne plates and Mieko places an oyster in front of me. The flesh retracts, a small, viscous lump. I take a deep breath and gulp it down.

Madame Ogawa seems satisfied. She asks me where I'm staying.

'Not far from here,' I reply, 'ten stations further north on the Yamanote line, at my grandparents' place.'

I pause. I feel awkward talking about my grandparents in Japanese. It makes them seem foreign somehow. I carry on talking, to compensate:

'They're Korean,' I say, 'they live in Nippori. They run a pachinko parlour there. It's only a small parlour, they've been running it for fifty years, ever since they arrived here.'

Mieko leans in towards the table, her lips closed. Madame Ogawa nods, a look of concern on her face, just as when I said I didn't do yoga. I can understand her reservations. Here in Japan, pachinko machines are seen as no different from casino slot machines. Everyone plays pachinko, but it's still disapproved of. Pachinko parlours have their own banking system, with a reputation for funding the main political parties under the counter. They advertise all over the media, feeding a whole parallel economy. But that's only the big chains like Diamond or Merrytale. Not small businesses like my grandfather's.

When we've finished eating, Madame Ogawa goes down to the pool, and Mieko sets her things out on the table.

'Aren't we going down to your room?' I ask.

'No, my mother's there.'

She calls me sensei, teacher in Japanese. I tell her to call me by my name, Claire, but it's hard for her to say; she pronounces it Calairo, so I ask her to use the Korean for big sister, onni.

'Onni,' she murmurs as if she's trying to commit it to memory.

Her homework is clearly set out in a notebook. Today's topic is agreement of French adjectives. I'm not

sure of her level, so I read the examples aloud for her, thinking what a dull textbook this is, colourless, with no pictures. Mieko knows it all perfectly, giving the answers before I can ask the questions.

'What's the point of me being here?' I ask her.

'We've practised it,' she says.

'Practised?'

'Yes, because you were coming.'

I think back to the meal we've just had, how everything she and her mother did was perfectly synchronised.

I watch her working through the exercises for a few moments and then leave her to get on with it. I walk over to the picture window, look down at the station; a central spine, four walkways fanning out like limbs. A lizard lying in wait. Buildings everywhere, overhead wires stretching into the distance, all the way to Mount Fuji, barely visible through the smog.

I scan the bookshelves. Rousseau, Chateaubriand. Essays on literature, Swiss Romantics. History books. The French Revolution. I have the feeling these books don't contain the history I learnt at school; these volumes tell of another parallel history, one that played out simultaneously on another planet.

Around one o'clock, Madame Ogawa comes back up with some royal milk tea and kkwabaegi, Korean doughnuts, from the Family Mart for us. The bodysuit she's wearing reveals every fold and pleat of her body.

After she's gone back down, I ask Mieko why her mother wears shoes inside the apartment. Japanese people usually take them off indoors.

'She says she needs to hear her own footsteps. I'm not supposed to tell anyone.'

We sit side by side munching our snacks. The label on the bottle of tea has a picture of Donald Duck and Daisy in their swimsuits, at the beach. A special summer offer. Of course, Disneyland Tokyo. I could take Mieko there. I'm not sure she'd like it, maybe amusement parks aren't her thing.

'Is there anywhere in particular you'd like me to take you while I'm here?'

She looks up at the ceiling, then at me, goes to say something, hesitates, sits up straight and eventually says she doesn't really mind, it's up to me. I feel vaguely annoyed. You're not much help, I think to myself.

When she's finished the worksheets, she asks me what she has to do next. I haven't prepared anything. I make up an exercise to keep her busy for a while.

I'm still feeling jet-lagged. Sitting on the sofa I have a hard time staying awake. There's not enough ventilation, the windows are steamed up, the room feels cramped. I'm bigger and bulkier than Mieko and her mother. If I'm not careful I might break something.

Walking me back to the lift, Madame Ogawa hands me an envelope and thanks me. She seems relieved that my visit is over. She's wearing a robe, her hair is wet. I haven't said goodbye to Mieko, she hasn't finished the worksheet. But the door slides shut.

I spend the train journey back to Nippori trying to dislodge a piece of kkwabaegi, stuck between my teeth. By the time I manage to work it free my tongue has started to bleed.

I ARRIVE at my grandparents' place to find my grand-mother seated on the floor in the living room surrounded by her Playmobil figures. She's removed all their hair. They smile vacantly.

'Where've you been?'

I don't answer, irritated by the whining tone she adopts whenever I come in. She knows perfectly well where I've been. She roots around in the pile of Playmobil wigs, pulls out one with a long braid and one with a bun, sets them on the heads of two female figures and holds them up to her ears, shaking them.

'Which one do you like best? I have to go to the hairdresser's.'

I take a good look at her. Long nose, rounded belly, like a baby seal.

'The bun.'

'Will you come with me?'

I call out yes from the kitchen. I put some water on to boil for the rice, soak the black beans. We'll eat when my grandfather gets home, at half past eight, after the pachinko parlour closes. He's ninety years old but he still goes every day, from dawn to dusk. I go back to the living room, open the window to let out the steam.

Nippori. Pale green, to match the green of the Yamanote line trains that slice through the neighbourhood on their elevated rails. Korean restaurants, Chinese noodles, sumo stables, the vast Yanaka cemetery up on the hill. And the pachinko parlours. Diamond and Merrytale on the street that goes to Nishi-Nippori; Shiny, my grand-father's, on the street leading to Uguisudani.

Our duplex is wedged between two tower blocks, across the street from the Shiny. You can see it from the kitchen and living-room windows, the gaudy front painted in red and white, like a clown's face. Now and then, the doors open to suck players in or spit them out with the smoke.

Shiny.

Not so shiny though, especially when you compare it with a Diamond or Merrytale. To attract customers, my grandfather employs a sandwich-board woman. She must be about my age. She stands on the corner by the taxi rank, at the foot of the steps leading up to the station, her two boards sporting the Shiny's colours clamped to her body. Her monotonous chant blends in with the piped music from the Family Mart, the convenience store next door, open twenty-four hours a day.

And then there's Yuki, scrawny and round-shouldered, in his pink sweater. The professional player hired to stand outside the Shiny in the morning, waiting for it to come to life. As soon as the doors open, he makes straight for the machine nearest the window. The idea is to create an impression of plenty. Come in, his presence says, inside the Shiny, things are buzzing.

At the front desk, the security guard with his surveillance cameras. A local policeman, retired. The Japanese government doesn't provide pensions for its employees. Men without savings or family to look after them in their old age have to go on working until the end of their lives. There aren't many pachinko parlours that don't have a retired policeman in charge of security.

WE EAT sitting on the floor at the low table in the living room. My grandfather raises his spoon slowly to his mouth, his hand shaking. Finally, he sucks in the contents in one gulp, as if the food he's carried so laboriously to his lips might evaporate. From time to time, he puts down his spoon and pours himself a glass of soju. He concentrates intently, his grip unsteady, but nothing spills. My grandmother leans over towards her bowl, slurping her food with gusto.

She looks up occasionally and asks me in English, 'Is good? Is good?'

'Ye, mashissoyo,' I mumble in Korean, 'yes, it's good.'

I sit facing them, trying to eat as slowly as my grandfather, delaying that moment at the end of the meal when a heavy silence descends.

They haven't mentioned our trip to Korea once since I arrived. We need to make plans, start buying tickets. I don't know how to raise the subject. I used to be able to speak Korean but I lost it when French became my main language. My grandfather used to correct my mistakes, but not any more. We communicate in simple English, with a few basic words in Korean and an array of gestures and exaggerated facial expressions. We never speak in Japanese.

When they turn on the television, I feign tiredness and go downstairs to my room. The staircase is narrow, like the one at Mieko's, except that here the floors are made of wood, the walls covered in mustard-coloured flock. My room is next to the bathroom. My grandparents use it to store bedding and extra tatami mats. When I was little the rolled-up bamboo mats standing sentinel in the half-light would appear in my dreams, transformed into giant grasshoppers.

The room is simply furnished. A bed, a desk, a few boxes of my mother's things. On top of one of the boxes

is our old Monopoly set, the Swiss edition my mother bought to give her parents an idea of where we live.

On the table by the bed iss a photo of my grandmother aged about ten, with plump cheeks and round belly, taken just before the Second World War. Her mother stands behind her, one hand on her shoulder. Dressed in the traditional white linen costume, they pose proudly. It was rare for women to have their picture taken in Seoul in those days. Over the years the white of their costume has taken on a dull tinge, a yellowish hue that speaks of mourning in both Korea and Japan.

I lie on the bed, wriggle out of my clothes. My feet protrude beyond the end of the bed. It's too hot. The polyester sheets cling to my stomach. In the end, I unroll one of the tatami mats, cover it with a sheet and lie on the ground, trying to find a cool spot.

Noises drift in from the street. Car exhausts, heels on the tarmac, and all night long, the sandwich-board woman's monotonous chant, relayed on playback through a loudspeaker.

The window is at street height. Lying on the ground, I can see people's legs as they hurry past, heading for the narrow streets of Uguisudani, where the love hotels are. I've never been inside one. I can't help thinking about the

girls who work there, the men in grey suits. Most of the girls are much younger than I am.

I picture the street. I know every inch of it, I've walked down it so often on my way to Ueno Park. The Schall, with its cut-out black bat on the roof. The Transatlantic. The Mont Blanc, with its jacuzzis. The Dream. Further along, you come to the bento box stall with its panda-shaped scales, walk over the bridge above the railway lines, pass the man in his makeshift canvas shelter, skirt along the cemetery as far as the whale statue in front of the Natural History Museum, and eventually arrive at Ueno Park. Starbucks, the University of the Arts, then the zoo.

Through the ceiling, I hear my grandmother laughing.

I open my laptop and check my emails. My friends gave up writing to me ages ago, I took too long to reply. Mathieu probably has too weak a signal. He's house-sitting a chalet in Val d'Anniviers, writing up his thesis. And my mother? Has she messaged me? She usually keeps me up to date on where my father's been playing. He's an organist. She sends me lists of the churches, chapels, cathedrals he's played in: Porrentruy, Zürich, Rheinau, Solothurn, Zollikon, Fribourg. She never gives me the programme, only the venue. I picture them both, dots on the map, hopping from town to village. How

easy it seems for them. Ever since I came to Japan I've felt drained of all energy. Sometimes when I read my mother's messages, I feel so exhausted I abandon whatever it was I was planning to do and stretch out on the bed, arms and legs spread, like a starfish.

She hasn't written.

My laptop starts making a loud whirring noise. I shut it down and become aware of the darkness. The silence in the house. I can't hear the television any more, nor my grandmother's laugh. Only the distant cry of the sandwich-board woman. I close my eyes and let sleep wash over me.

THREE DAYS have gone by. I've changed my mind about taking Mieko to Disneyland. All children love places like that. I'd have gone there myself with my grandmother when I was Mieko's age, but my mother was against it. She didn't consider it appropriate.

I head towards Nippori station. It's rained in the night, a monsoon downpour, although Japan's monsoon season is supposed to be over. The temperature has stalled, several degrees above the average for this time of year.

The sandwich-board woman smells of wet clothes. Her boards are limp and waterlogged. She's stepped back

under the awning, out of the rain, but still visible from the sidewalk. Her hair is matted. She fixes her gaze straight ahead, the microphone in her hand. It's supposed to be attached to her cap. The elastic must have gone. I make a mental note to mention it to my grandfather.

It's not quite time for my train. I go into the Family Mart, stop in front of the packaged pastries, try to get a clearer image of the contents obscured by the logos all over the packaging. I can see someone squinting at the yoghurts in the chilled section. Pink sweater. Yuki. I ran into him here this morning too. He comes in by the back entrance, through the glass door that connects with the Shiny.

Most players at this time of day are women; they come while their children are at school, or on summer programmes, and their husbands are at work. The older people, retirees, come mostly in the afternoon. Early in the evening, the machines are taken over by salarymen and sumo wrestlers.

Yuki selects a choco-mint doughnut and goes back to the Shiny. The door slides open; a blast of loud music, rapid-fire salvos of pachinko balls. People say the name pachinko comes from the noise the balls make in the machine, pinging against the glass, swooshing through

the plastic tubes, clanking against the bumpers, the shriek of metal, the final clang as they fall into the tray.

The door slides shut.

Silence.

Yuki takes his seat at his usual machine, rips the wrapping from the doughnut, eats it with one hand, the other hand poised on the lever. He gazes out of the window.

The rules are simple. The player sits in front of the upright pachinko machine and feeds money in. Balls come spurting up, thousands of metal balls – spraying, tumbling and bouncing off a series of obstacles, all the way down to the bottom of the vertical playing field, then vanishing into one of three holes. Balls that fall into the middle hole come back out in a cart on the outside of the machine. Players can exchange them for prizes at the end of the session, the prize lots determined by the number of balls.

The only control a player has over the machine is to adjust the force at which the balls are ejected by slowly turning a knob that fits into the palm of the hand. The knob turns both ways. There's not much else for players to do. Some jam the knob into position with a coin, leaving their hands free so they can smoke. The experienced players keep one hand on the handle. That

way they can stay in control, sense the slightest hitch,
tweak the handle in response or relax the fingers a little.
The smallest of movements, almost imperceptible, can
influence the outcome. They stay focused, ignoring the
flashing lights, the other players, the cigarette burning
down, the wail of the piped music and the din of the
three hundred pachinko machines in my grandfather's
gaming hall.

At a quarter past eight, I buy some plums and a couple
of doughnuts, walk to the station, the sandwich-board
woman's cry in my ears:

'Shiny and bright, shiny and bright, shiny Shiny every
night . . .'

DOMED BLUE CEILING, a phantom ocean. The Little Mermaid hangs from a wire, waving her hands in greeting, her tail swishing sinuously in her wake. Her stomach bulges from the harness beneath her bodysuit. Down on the ground, visitors brandish cameras, contorting themselves to keep her in their sights. A puff of smoke and Triton, king of the waves, surges forth. A robot, not a living actor like the mermaid. His voice booms out a warning to his daughter: 'Moray eels.' Ariel screams, another puff of smoke, she spins one last time and disappears. Darkness.

Outside, it's raining again.

'Did you like that?' I ask Mieko, nervously.

'Yes.'

Minnie Mouse is handing out ponchos and pink umbrellas. People are starting to line the main street. Clustered together, all swathed in plastic, they remind me of bubble wrap.

'What are we waiting for?' I ask Mieko, realising we've joined the expectant crowd.

'The parade.'

She's too far back to be able to see anything.

'Do you want to stand in front of me?' I ask.

'I don't mind.'

I ask her what she'd like to do. She scans the scene. I suggest It's a Small World, there's no queue there at the moment. She pulls a face.

What about the Haunted Mansion? Another grimace.

'Peter Pan's Flight?'

'Okay.'

I suspect she's only saying yes to please me.

'Or something else, if you prefer.'

'No, that's fine.'

We fly over London, the city set out beneath us, children's bedrooms, Big Ben displaying midnight. It's warm

and clammy in our pirate ship, there's a smell of sweat. I try not to touch any surfaces. The seat belt is loose on Mieko, even when it's pulled tight. I can't see the expression on her face. When we get to the pirates' island, I make a show of laughing at Captain Hook, oohing and aahing exaggeratedly until suddenly we pick up speed and I'm flung against Mieko. She turns and gives me a slightly condescending smile. For the rest of the ride, I cling to the edge of the seat.

When we emerge it's raining even harder. We wait it out in the souvenir shop. A father with his two sons. He tells them they can each choose a soft toy. Australian accent. He reminds me of Mathieu, with that sweater, the orange anorak. Mathieu has started talking about children lately. There don't seem to be many here. It's mostly young couples. The man smiles at me, he's seen me looking at him. He must think I'm a parent too. I look away.

Mieko is examining the Minnie Mouse ears.

'Would you like a pair of ears?' I ask.

She shakes her head. Does she want a drink? No. I adjust my poncho. I'm thirsty. I need something to drink. I tell her to wait for me here.

I cross the road, make for a café inside Ali Baba's Cavern. Minnie Mouse is there too, on a break. She's removed the head of her costume, the big hands. I sip my drink slowly, relieved to be away from Mieko. I want her to enjoy herself. Have some fun. I feel like tugging at her ear, pinching her cheek and pleading directly into her ear: please, Mieko, please have fun.

The Australian has followed me. He's seated the boys at a table near mine and gone to give their order. A waitress approaches him, hands him a menu in English, passes one to the French couple too, and to those young Chinese girls. I wasn't offered one, people think I'm Japanese. But I've never felt more foreign than I have this summer, with this child at my side.

The father comes back with a tray of cinnamon rolls. His children fall on them hungrily. I scurry away to rejoin Mieko.

I find her stroking a Bambi figurine.

'Do you like Bambi?' I ask hopefully.

She nods.

'Would you like me to buy it for you?'

'No, that's okay.'

'I'll give it to you as a gift. I'd like to.'

'But I don't want it. His mother's dead and his father goes away somewhere at the end, and we don't know where he's gone.'

'That's because he's old. He goes away to die.'

'I know that,' she says scathingly.

Snippets of the story come back to me. It wasn't my favourite Disney tale, I found it irritating, the timid little fawn afraid of his own shadow.

'I don't want it!' she says again as I head towards the cash desk with the figurine.

'I'm buying it for my grandmother.'

She stares at me in disbelief. I finish paying and stuff the figurine into the bottom my bag, holding it close under my arm to keep it out of the rain. Mieko hasn't taken her eyes off me.

'It's just to remind her of when I was little,' I say, thinking of the evenings my grandmother and I used to spend together watching the videos I brought with me from Switzerland – The Lion King, The Little Mermaid, Sleeping Beauty – it was something we both enjoyed.

'All children play with their grandmothers . . .'

'I didn't,' she mutters, eyes cast down.

I try and make amends. I wasn't exactly playing with my grandmother, I say, it was more a way of being

together, and besides, I didn't see her very often, only during the holidays, and my grandfather was always working at the pachinko parlour, from morning till night.

'The pachinko parlour,' Mieko says, interrupting me. 'That's where I'd like to go.'

I laugh. Does she even know what a pachinko parlour is? She rolls her eyes. Obviously, everyone knows about pachinko parlours, they're everywhere. She's never been inside one. That's what she wants to do with me.

'They're not for children you know, it's not a children's game.'

'I know.'

She stares at me earnestly. I doubt my grandfather would object to me showing her round the Shiny. It'd certainly be less bother and much less expensive than coming all this way out of the city to Disneyland. Even so, I don't want to make any promises.

'If you like, one day . . . Maybe we could, yes.'

Mieko smiles. At long last, I think to myself, she looks like a normal kid.

In the restaurant in the Star Wars section, Mieko orders omurice and I have a raspberry tart. We sit by the window.

The parade is in full flow. Ariel, Cinderella, Minnie Mouse, Mickey Mouse and Donald Duck file past, one by one, waving their arms in the air to the jolly music and lip-syncing the words to 'Happiness Is Here', all jigging about, even the actors (slaves perhaps?) tethered to Aladdin's float. On every face the same tightly stretched grin, the same vacant, happy look.

Mieko goes on eating, paying them no attention.

'Is that good?'

'It's filling.'

I look down at my tart. A single raspberry glistens atop a lump of whipped cream. Compact and rubbery-looking. I pick up my knife, cut the tart into sections and start eating. It tastes fatty. I spit it out into my napkin. The raspberry stares up at me, still intact, coated in a film of jelly.

MY GRANDFATHER is spooning his food into his mouth faster than usual. He spills some soju, pushes away the napkin I offer him. My grandmother has already left the table and is sitting on the sofa pretending to read a magazine. She went missing yesterday, while I was out at Disneyland. She set off by train for Shin-Okubo, where the Korean shops are, in search of long noodles. She didn't recognise the station and stayed on the train, going round and round on the Yamanote line over and over again. My grandfather assumed I was with her. I called the police as soon as I got home. You need to wait for a while, they said, old people are unpredictable,

they often act on a whim. In the end, a Japan Railways employee brought her back home; he'd found her in one of the seats reserved for elderly people, asleep.

'All that for a few noodles,' my grandfather grumbles.

'I'll go with her next time,' I say under my breath.

'I can go by myself,' my grandmother protests.

Looking at them, I feel overwhelmed. Their lives begin and end with the pachinko parlour. The only social interactions they have are to do with exchanging balls for trinkets: one hundred balls, a bottle of water; one thousand balls, a bar of chocolate; ten thousand balls, an electric razor; no balls, a pack of chewing gum, the consolation prize. They don't socialise at all with other Zainichis, Japan's Korean community: exiles, people who came, as my grandparents did, to escape the Korean war, and others, who were deported during the Japanese occupation of Korea.

'We need to organise things for the trip,' I say tentatively, almost to myself. 'I still haven't booked our tickets.'

My grandfather complains that he can't leave the pachinko parlour in the middle of the season. I remind him that we'd planned to go for one week only, at the beginning of September. He'll think it over, he says. We can discuss it again tomorrow. It's time for the service.

And slipping into a well-established routine, my grandparents push the coffee table to one side and place two cushions in front of the television set tuned to KBS World, the Korean channel that broadcasts the weekly church service. They sit cross-legged on the floor, Bibles in hand, following along attentively. When it's time for the hymns they both join in the singing, my grandmother's voice strong and full, my grandfather's a wavering vibrato. My grandmother looks up, lost; my grandfather helps her find her place, keeping time with his index finger. They're completely absorbed, unaware of my presence.

On the table, our three bowls make the shape of a face. My grandparents', the two eyes; mine, the mouth, rounded as if in astonishment. I clear them away and get on with the washing up. When I've finished, I help myself to a beer and go downstairs to my room. I'll have to stop doing this soon. I can't go on using jet lag as an excuse for knocking myself out like this for much longer.

My mother has messaged me. My birthday is still two weeks away but she wanted to make sure I read this in time. They love me lots, I'm their pet, their little chicken, they send me hugs.

There's an audio attachment. A clip from a radio programme, a recording of the classical music festival in Verbier. An organ solo, in a church. A piece I don't know. The last few bars. A pause. People clap, the organ strikes up again. It's playing 'Happy Birthday'. The commentator is surprised, mumbles something about it apparently being someone's birthday today, urges everyone to celebrate with the unknown person. The applause grows louder. Someone shouts: 'Hooray.'

There's a picture with the message. My father, at the organ, photographed from behind, my mother in the foreground, a selfie. She's smiling, features distorted by the perspective: double chin, mouth enlarged, forehead shrunk.

I take a good look at the picture. Swipe it away quickly to save it.

I have a message from Mathieu too. He's in the village, he's come down the mountain to send me this message. He says he misses me, he thinks I'd like the chalet, you can lie in bed and gaze at the Dent Blanche. Has my grandfather managed to reduce his hours? He's concerned about my grandmother's health. He's thinking of us, sends them his love.

I feel reassured by the tone of his message. He's not angry with me after our parting words at the airport.

He'd said not to worry, if I had any problems at all he'd come straight over, I could count on him. I'd snapped at him, said they were my grandparents, not his, insisted everything would be fine and gone through security without looking back.

But it was his caring nature that had attracted me to him in the first place, when I was in his Japanese seminar class at Geneva University. From the start, Mathieu had tried to understand the reason for my lack of enthusiasm. I told him it was Korean I really wanted to study, but to do that, I'd have to go to Berlin, London, Paris. I couldn't do it in Switzerland. I never went, I couldn't imagine being so far away from home. I fell back on Japanese, telling myself it would make my visits to my grandparents easier.

'You can learn Korean later,' Mathieu used to say.

It was all so easy for him. My grandparents spoke Japanese with him. We went to see them together twice. His presence masked the difficulties I had in communicating. Mathieu would spend whole days with my grandmother. I'd go for walks all over the neighbourhood while they were together. I felt relieved, but I was jealous too. He'd report their conversations to me in the evenings, in this room; they talked mostly about their life in Korea, before, under Japanese occupation.

'They made it illegal to speak Korean. You could be sentenced to death for speaking it. And do you know what your grandmother's mother did to avoid being subjected to speaking Japanese at school? She sliced off part of her own tongue.'

I didn't know. I knew almost nothing about my grandparents' past. They didn't talk about it with me or my mother. I knew they'd come to Japan by sea in 1952 to escape the civil war in Korea when they were eighteen and nineteen years old, my grandmother pregnant with my mother. They'd heard rumours of a flourishing industry in Japan, run by Zainichis. There was nothing in the way of entertainment in those post-war days: no cinema, no theatre. The black market was everywhere, with cigarettes the most prized commodity. Koreans were locked out of the Japanese labour market by virtue of their nationality. So, they invented a game: vertical tray, metal balls, a lever. And cigarettes in exchange for balls.

It was Mathieu who explained to me how important pachinko became to the Japanese economy. In 1953, while Korea was tearing itself apart, its people fleeing to wherever they could, there were almost four hundred thousand pachinko parlours in Japan. Interest waned

during the 1960s when other forms of entertainment began to expand, but even now there are still more than twenty thousand pachinko parlours in Japan, all run exclusively by Zainichis and their descendants.

Mathieu found it surprising that in all those years of exile, my grandparents had never returned to Korea. I remember, when I was little, hearing them say they'd go back one day. Now that they'd reached such a great age, we decided it would be best for us to take them there. It was up to Mathieu to speak to them about it. He said they seemed keen, and we booked our flights to Tokyo. Korea was unfamiliar territory for both of us and we were planning to make all the other arrangements once we arrived in Tokyo. But as the time approached, Mathieu realised he still had a great deal of work to do to finish his thesis. Eventually he decided to pull out of the trip, but he encouraged me to go without him. I couldn't see myself reading his drafts on the family unit in Japan during the twelfth century – I'd just finished working on a second Master's degree myself. So, I came to Tokyo on my own.

Footsteps on the stairs. I'd left my door open. My grand-father walks past my room, in his pyjamas, waves hello,

goes into the bathroom. He's probably seen the beer. I close the door, turn off the light, lie down on the floor. I start a game of Tetris on my phone. The screen flashes in the darkness. Headlights from passing cars light up the room intermittently. I think about the photo of my parents again, my mother's message. Me as their little chicken. I picture myself running round in circles, banging into things, falling over. Clucking. I try not to giggle.

I FIND MIEKO sitting in a corner of the empty pool, arms wrapped round her knees, gazing despondently at an upturned plastic bowl. She's not moving at all, except for her lips, which are opening and closing, making a gentle popping sound, like a bubble bursting. There's a bee under the bowl; she found it buzzing around the pool a few days ago. She trapped it, afraid it might sting her, and now she's scared of looking under the bowl.

I lift it carefully.

The bee is stuck to the rim of the bowl, dried out. I give it a shake. It slips off and as it hits the ground, its wings and legs fall off.

'I'm horrible,' Mieko wails.

I place my hand on her shoulder.

'These things happen . . .'

'You don't understand,' she retorts. 'I wanted it to die. I wanted it dead. I'm a horrible person.'

She taps her head feebly against the side of the pool, saying over and over again that she's horrible, horrible.

I go back up to the bathroom and flush the dead creature down the toilet. Watching it whirl around the bowl it occurs to me that I'm used to seeing bees in Switzerland. But not here. Where did it come from?

When I come back down, Mieko is lying flat on her stomach on the bed, completely still, her face buried in the pillow, hidden beneath her helmet of black hair. The thought that she might be dead flashes through my mind.

'You think this room is weird,' she blurts out, her voice muffled by the pillow.

'What?'

She turns and looks up, red-faced.

'You look at it like you think it's weird.'

I try and deny it but she says she hates it too, and I immediately regret lying to her.

'Can you swim?' I ask.

She says she wishes she'd learnt, but her mother thinks the water in swimming pools isn't clean, it's full of bacteria, it's not good for your digestion. I say she's not missing much, I've never really liked swimming.

'You don't like pachinko too,' she says. 'You don't like anything.'

'Pachinko either. We say "either". And that's not what I said. It's not true that I don't like anything.'

'Why aren't we going there?'

'We will,' I say.

'When?'

'Soon.'

'Promise?'

'I promise,' I say unconvincingly.

I set today's lesson out on the desk. This time I've prepared the exercises. Mieko says she's hungry and I produce the plums and kkwabaegi I bought at the Family Mart from my bag.

'Doughnuts!' she exclaims. 'My favourite!'

She breaks open a plum and plants it on a doughnut. It looks like a stick figure sitting cross-legged.

'Me, with fair hair,' she says waving it about next to her face.

'Stop it, you look like my grandmother.'

She bursts out laughing, says she can't wait to meet her.

'I'm not sure we'll be able to do that,' I say cautiously.

'Why? When we go to the pachinko parlour . . .'

'She's never there. It's only my grandfather. She stays at home. Whenever she goes out, she gets lost.'

'Why? Doesn't she know her way around?'

'She's old. And no, Tokyo isn't really her home.'

Mieko purses her lips, a sign that she's processing this. My grandmother wouldn't like the idea of this meeting at all, I think to myself. She'd have to speak Japanese.

'Did she like your Bambi gift?' Mieko asks.

I mumble yes, ask her if she has any coloured felt-tips, I can't find any in her desk drawers.

'You know,' she says, 'I saw some fawns once. In Miyajima. There are loads of them wandering about, but people feed them and they're getting a bit stupid and starting to die. They're forgetting how to find food for themselves. Or else they get diabetes.'

Miyajima. The island famous for its shrine at the water's edge, with the red gates that seem to float on the

water at high tide. Mathieu had wanted to go there, but we ended up just staying at my grandparents' place.

'I went there by train with my daddy. We were right up front with the driver. My dad was checking to see everything was working properly – he designed the train. I never fed the deer. But there was still one that followed me. Everywhere I went, even in the morning outside the hotel, it'd been waiting for me all night.'

I tease her, was it really the same one? With so many of them, how could she be sure? She looks taken aback, her eyes well up.

'I was only joking,' I say quickly.

She props herself up on her elbows.

'One day I'll have a real bedroom. But we can't leave while Daddy's still not here.'

'Where is he?'

'Don't you know? He got on a train one day and he's never come back.'

I turn and look at her. She's flung herself back down onto the mattress. I think back to what I said to her at Disneyland, about Bambi, his father going away to die.

'I'm so sorry, Mieko. I had no idea.'

She says it doesn't matter, it happened a long time ago. And then adds:

'But if we're not here when he comes back, how would he ever find us?'

She sighs, a long exhale that turns into a hissing sound. I feel awkward and suggest we do some work.

'What does your dad do?' she asks.

I tell her about the organ, the teaching, the church services, the concerts. Mieko listens attentively, asks how an organ works. I can't explain, I don't really know much about it. Rather tersely, I say:

'Come along now. We have work to do.'

She drags herself over to the desk.

Instead of working from Mieko's book we practise a dialogue I've made up. I couldn't face the Japanese manual so I scoured my memory for inspiration and came up with a simple conversation between a girl and a boy. I've sketched them in felt-tips. I start:

'Hello, Carol, I'm Martin. Do you want to play with me?'

'Why not?' Mieko replies.

I try not to laugh. Her voice has a nasal twang when she speaks French. It makes me feel less intimidated.

'All right, come on then! What shall we play?'

I stare at her, waiting for her to reply:

'Go on,' I say. 'Your turn.'

She frowns, says I've just stolen her line. I say it doesn't matter.

'So am I supposed to be the girl now?' she asks.

'The girl or the boy. It's all the same.'

She flings herself against the back of her chair.

'I can't.'

'You're doing fine. Go on, read it.'

She stares at me. 'You're not really a teacher anyway.'

'French is my first language.'

'I thought it was Japanese.'

'Of course it isn't. How could it be? My great-grandmother sliced off her tongue so she wouldn't have to speak Japanese!'

I stick out my tongue and make a cutting motion: 'Like this. With a knife.'

'That must hurt,' Mieko says, grimacing.

'Must *have* hurt. She's dead.'

I give her a stern look. She sets to work, and I sit on the bed in her spot. I shouldn't have lost my temper like that. She's too young to understand, it has nothing to do with her. We agree to give up on manuals and exercises and just chat instead, in French or in Japanese, whatever we feel like.

'You won't tell your mother?'

'Yes, I won't tell.'

We spend the rest of the afternoon playing Tetris on my phone. I can't concentrate. I keep thinking of the photo my mother sent me. It worries me. She looks older, she's ageing. I've never noticed it before.

'We'll go and see some deer if you like,' I say to Mieko. 'Real ones.'

'Where?'

'At the zoo. In Ueno Park. It's near where my grand-parents live.'

Her face lights up.

'Okay.'

When Madame Ogawa comes home, Mieko chats to her about her day. I feel out of place and shut myself in the bathroom. Dust has been left to accumulate. No beauty products. Only soap, and a shampoo base. I wash my hands. I feel tainted. All that rain has stirred up the pollutants, the air is heavy with them. Toxins seep into my body through every pore, leak out in my sweat. The

earth expelling poison through the humans it wears on its surface like a coat of hairs.

I go back out and find Madame Ogawa sitting by herself on the sofa. She pats the seat beside her, inviting me to join her. She asks me how the visit to Disneyland went. I embellish things a little, make it sound like Mieko and I get on better than we do.

'She's a lonely child,' she says eventually. 'I'm glad she likes you.'

I smile, out of politeness.

'What do you think of her French?'

'It's good.'

I ask her why she hasn't taken on one of her students as a tutor for Mieko.

'I teach literature, not language,' she replies. 'And in any case, with my students, it would complicate matters, you understand . . . Having them come here.'

'Of course.'

She gives a half-smile.

'And besides, it was an opportunity to meet you. I'd like to send Mieko to Switzerland later, to a French school.'

She tells me she went to university in Switzerland. She found the experience profoundly enjoyable.

'Have you read *Heidi*?' she asks, scanning the bookshelves with her eyes.

I try and remember the story. My mother must have read it to me. I have a vague memory of something rather old-fashioned, about a little girl.

'I saw the cartoon long before I realised it was actually a book,' Madame Ogawa continues. 'I was sure it was Japanese. Johanna Spyri suffered from depression – but you must know this, you live in Switzerland.'

I mumble something about not being aware of it.

She continues, 'She couldn't write the book until after she'd brought up her children. Do you have children?'

'No,' I reply hastily.

She gives me a sidelong glance.

'If you do become a mother, I hope for your sake you don't have a daughter. She'll start comparing herself with you eventually. It's inevitable.'

She picks up a folder full of photos, flips through them and takes one out.

'So much open space . . .' she says, waving the picture around as if it might help her remember something.

She passes me the photo. I recognise the tram junction, the green-tiled steeple. Paradeplatz in Zürich. It makes

me think of Monopoly, my grandmother trying to find the town where we lived on the board. My mother and I had covered up the last square, Zürich Paradeplatz, for fun, and written Yverdon-les-Bains on it in indelible felt-tip. Our own Pestalozzi Square, transformed into the most expensive real estate in Europe.

'You see,' I'd explained to my grandmother, who didn't understand why we were laughing, 'it's as if Mum was saying that we live in like, I don't know, Manhattan, or the Champs-Élysées in Paris.'

'Okay,' she said, 'Paris, okay, okay, Paris . . .'

Madame Ogawa pulls out more photos and waves them about in the same way before showing them to me. Lausanne Cathedral, the Federal Palace, the Bear Pit.

'You see,' she says, 'I can't send Mieko over there until she's mastered the language.'

'She can learn it while she's there . . .'

'No, that's out of the question. The standard in Swiss schools is very high, she wouldn't be able to keep up.'

Her voice hardens. 'Perhaps she'd never be able to fit in. Like you, here. You'll never really be able to speak Japanese, will you?'

I'm speechless. Every conversation we've had has been in Japanese. I try to catch her eye but she's turned away to look out the bay window. The city is suffused

with light, Mount Fuji drained of colour. The sun's last rays filter through the spaces between buildings.

'I didn't know your parents ran a pachinko parlour,' she says eventually.

'My grandparents. Why would you know?'

'Couldn't they find work where they lived?'

'In Korea?'

She inclines her head as if to say yes, of course.

'Gambling's illegal in Korea. They're fine here. They have plenty of work.'

I choose my words carefully. Gambling for money is illegal in Japan too. Pachinko isn't seen as gambling because the balls are exchanged for sweets, toilet paper, bottles of water, toothpaste. Or dominoes. People swap them for money once they leave the parlour. Anonymously, through a hole in the wall, somewhere near the pachinko parlour.

'They must miss their country.'

'No, they don't,' I lie.

'And it's so close. Barely a two-hour flight,' she presses on.

'It's not as simple as that.'

Although it is, I think to myself. My grandparents would never fly, but they could go by train, by boat. Tokyo.

Nagoya. Kyoto. Shin-Osaka. Hiroshima, Hakata. Three hours by ferry to Busan, train to Seoul. Simple.

Madame Ogawa shuffles the photos:

'I have nothing against pachinko as such. But children are often left in the street while their mothers are playing, and when things don't go so well for the parents, their children sometimes have to go without food.'

'It's not like that at my grandparents',' I say, humiliated at being forced to defend them.

'Of course not.'

She goes to say something, hesitates. I'm tempted to say more, to invent stories about gangsters, but I can understand why she thinks the way she does. I make a point of assuring her that I won't take her daughter there, fully aware that I've just promised Mieko the opposite.

Visibly relieved, Madame Ogawa turns to the window. I can see from our reflections that she's trying not to look at me. She gazes off into the distance, somewhere towards Tokyo Tower, the one shaped like the Eiffel Tower.

'In the end, it's no worse than . . . Nippori's not such a bad place to live. The hillside is stable, safe from earthquakes. That's why they built the cemetery there.'

'Mieko told me about her father.'

Silence.

'What did she tell you?'

'Not much.'

Madame Ogawa smiles sadly.

'You know, in Japan, thousands of people disappear every year. There are businesses you can go to, to get a new identity.'

She turns back to face me.

'I'm telling you this to avoid misunderstandings. It has nothing to do with Mieko, nor with me. His leaving like that, you know, it wasn't . . . a betrayal.'

I look out of the window. Mount Fuji is shrouded in darkness now. The city has become no more than a leaden mass, lifeless. Lines are starting to blur inside the apartment too. I feel as though I can hardly move. Without the view from the window, it would be unbearable. You'd suffocate. I have a sudden image of Mathieu, in his cabin.

'It was lovely today,' I say. 'We could see Mount Fuji.'

'Oh, yes?'

Madame Ogawa takes a step towards the window.

'I hate being up this high. It makes me dizzy. I like it when it's foggy. When you can't see into the distance. When there's no horizon. It gives me a feeling of having time. That it's all right not to see, not to be aware of what's in my path.'

She gives a short laugh.

'When you think about it . . . about trains . . . we should really build ships and learn to live on the water.'

She flicks the light switch and the furniture takes shape again.

I stand up.

'I think I'll go.'

'You're not staying? To eat with us, I mean. I bought some oysters.'

'My grandparents are expecting me . . .'

She asks me to give her a moment, goes into the kitchen and comes back with a jar of greyish liquid for me.

'For your grandparents. They're marinated.'

As I stuff the jar into my bag I notice the oysters floating in the liquid, their frilly edges stained by soy sauce. Madame Ogawa presses the button for the lift. I say goodbye, addressing her as sensei. She corrects me. I should call her Henriette, she says hurriedly, as if to dispel a momentary embarrassment.

'Henriette,' I say.

LEANING AGAINST the wall of the carriage, I watch the other passengers' reflections in the window opposite. A teenager hunched over his phone, headphones clamped to his ears. Three young women in heels. One of them is putting on her make-up, using her friend's glasses as a mirror. Another pulls on a grey tutu over her suit, peeling off the suit afterwards. Some of the men watch. It's Saturday evening, I'd forgotten. Further down, another young woman. Round face, soft arms. Her trousers don't fit, they're too long for her. I adjust my stance and realise I've made myself conspicuous. I straighten up, act like I'm playing Tetris to hide my embarrassment.

I think about what Madame Ogawa – Henriette – said. About pachinko and the Shiny. The sequins. The glitter ball. My mother always did her best to keep me away from it during our visits. We used to come for two or three weeks a year, it was the only time I spent with grandparents. I remember the players smelling of grilled meat, cigarettes. How cold it was in winter when the doors swung open. The piped music. The silent players, deep in concentration, sweating. The machines constantly spitting out balls, absorbing the occasional blow. I felt almost affectionate towards those machines, a kind of pity tinged with fear. As soon as they were fed, their contents would be regurgitated, undigested.

My grandfather still had hair then, always carefully combed with the same wax that sumo wrestlers use. He let me arrange the prizes in the display, making sure my mother didn't know about it. Every evening, he'd go round checking all the machines, taking note of any in need of repair, making sure nothing could go wrong.

There was one incident. A player fed a coin into his machine's rumbling belly. Nothing happened. No balls appeared. He put in another coin. The machine spat it out, 'Error' flashed up on the screen. He stared. The screen blinked. Once. Twice. Went dead. He called for

my grandfather, who offered him another machine to play while he repaired the first one. But the player started shouting about this being his machine, it was the only one he ever played. He wrapped his arms round it, as if trying to breathe life into it. My grandfather tried to reason with him, but the man still clung to the pachinko machine, like a tick to its host. When my grandfather threatened to call the police, the man began to cry. I was scared and hid by the desk, behind the crates of fizzy drinks. He ended up punching the screen, accusing my grandfather of being a crook and screaming that the machine had been tampered with. The security guard was in on it too, he shouted, they were dogs, every one of them. He left before he had a chance to see the machine spitting out an endless stream of balls. They spurted out of every hole, rolling unchecked along the ground, rebounding against the other machines, against players' feet, until finally they rolled to a stop against the wall.

My grandfather picked them up one by one and put them back into the machine, moving with his customary lack of haste. The other players paid no attention. Once he'd finished he came to find me in my hiding place. Sensing my confusion, he looked me in the eyes and said no one was to blame. Machines sometimes went wrong.

Back then, they were manually operated. Now, they're all computerised.

I get back to Nippori at seven o'clock in the evening. The sky is charcoal grey. Crows circle above the electric wires. Outside the Chinese restaurant, people are queuing.

'Shiny, Shiny, day and night, shiny, Shiny, shining bright.'

I notice the microphone attached to the sandwich-board woman's baseball cap. Her shoes. White trainers, laced up like mine, with double bows. She turns her head slightly towards me. I pretend to be studying the machines. Yuki is on one near the window. I can see the guard behind the counter, facing the CCTV monitors, the top of my grandfather's head as he bends to look at something. I'd go in and say hello, see what's new in the displays, the prizes he's offering, but my mind is on that conversation with Henriette. I can't stop thinking about Mieko. I go into the Family Mart instead and buy a doughnut.

SHIN-OKUBO, Tokyo's Koreatown. Life-size cut-outs of pop singers and soap stars, shops selling cosmetics. The pavements heave with Japanese teenagers. Food trucks stretch for a hundred metres, Japanese teens queue for dakkochi. A spicy, caramel smell. Shin-Okubo, one long skewer of grilled chicken.

We've walked the entire length of the street without finding my grandmother's usual hair salon. Traffic sweeps past on the main road, the towers of stylish Shinjuku rising on the other side. My grandmother wants to cross the road, keep searching. I tell her we've come to the end of Koreatown, the salon must have closed down, we need to turn back.

'You don't like my hair anyway,' my grandmother grumbles. 'You're always giving me that funny look.'

'That's nonsense,' I say.

I apologise immediately. I'm overtired. It's the heat. The sandwich-board woman. I can't stand it, she keeps me awake at night. The loudspeaker crackling. My grandmother tugs at my sleeve and says something in my ear. I should treat the girl nicely. She used to work in a bar as a hostess. Her father came in drunk one evening. He made advances to her, not realising she was his own daughter. She pushed him away and he broke a bottle over her head.

'She's a bit soft in head, you know,' my grandmother says, tapping at her temple. 'We've had her since January.'

'She must get so cold,' I mutter.

'Your grandfather turns on the heat.'

'Yes, with those enormous boards, I'm sure she's well insulated.'

'Aigou, yeppun sekhi, poor little thing, poor little thing,' she wails, my sarcastic remark completely lost on her.

I steer her towards the most brightly coloured boutique, regretting it as soon as I see the trendy clients. A woman with pink hair ushers her to a seat and asks how she can be of help. My grandmother wants a black

tint. With a streak of blue. The stylist glances at me for approval.

'Blue,' my grandmother says again.

Whatever I say she'll be cross. I bury my head in a magazine.

While her hair is being shampooed she starts to talk. The stylist nods. My grandmother is getting excited. She's talking about me, boasting of my linguistic prowess, counting off languages on her fingers. She says I speak French, German, English, Italian. She's exaggerating, I cringe. She mentions Switzerland, 'seuwisseu, seuwisseu'. The girl pretends to be impressed. When my grandmother starts boasting about how good my Korean is, I can't take any more. I stand up.

'Are you leaving me?' she asks, worried.

I mumble something about coming back soon.

Outside, I close my eyes, turn my face to the sun. Dots of light form beneath my lids. I stand there like that for a moment, dazzled.

Not so long ago my grandmother was still playing the face game with me. She'd stick plasters all over my face and then ask me to say the words: *ipp*, mouth; *noun*,

eye; *theok*, chin; *ipsul*, lips; *kho*, nose. With each correct answer she would delicately peel off some of the plasters.

'That's how you discover a face, your little round face, the most beautiful face in the world, my granddaughter, my little girl, my cupcake, my baby, my big sweetie-pie with the little round face.'

She'd laugh and stroke my face. But one evening, when I'd stumbled over the vocabulary several times, she ripped all the plasters off at once, pulling so roughly I felt my skin burning, saying that if I forgot these words, I'd be stuck like that forever, with plaster all over my face, like a mummy.

I go to the supermarket and buy fish stock, kimchi, the noodles she wanted and a tube of sweetened condensed milk. I've noticed that she likes it, she licks a tube of it before she goes to bed, after she's brushed her teeth.

On my way back to the hairdresser's I see her on the street. She's looking around frantically, trying to find me. Her hair is still damp.

'Where were you?' she hisses as I walk up to her.

'Didn't she dry your hair?'

'You walked off. I walked out too, I didn't like that girl. Where were you?'

'Guess what!' I say, holding up the bag of shopping. 'I bought you some noodles.'

'I wanted to get them myself. Which ones did you buy?'

She starts rummaging in the bag.

'Condensed milk! I didn't know you liked it too! You never said!'

We walk back to the station, my grandmother beaming happily. She hangs on to my arm. We stumble along, out of step with each other, her blue streak fluttering at my shoulder.

'Did you pay the stylist?' I ask suddenly.

'Eh? I'm a thief now, am I?'

Inside the station she tells me her train pass has run out of credit. The machine is out of order, we need to go to the ticket window. She glances up at the station employee, hesitates, hands me the card.

'You go. I can't see what I'm doing.'

We exchange looks. I know she's not telling the truth. She doesn't want to go the ticket window because she'll have to speak Japanese. She waits for me in a corner of the concourse, staring at her hands.

On the platform I ask her if she and my grandfather have thought ahead to when they can't run the pachinko parlour any more. My grandmother brushes away my concern, irritated. She's worked it out. They'd be able to live for four years on their savings. And in any case, with her old bones, she won't last long, and have I seen my grandfather, he'll die before her, and if he dies, she will too. I look at her in shock. She laughs, says she was joking. I insist. Seriously. They might fall, the stairs in their house are steep. Couldn't they move, delegate the management of the Shiny to the security guard perhaps? She says my grandfather is fine, but the security guard on the other hand is half-dead, plus he wouldn't be able to afford it, he's Japanese.

I'd forgotten. The steep taxes Japanese people have to pay when it comes to pachinko. Zainichi Koreans are exempt.

'I could always make doughnuts,' my grandmother declares. 'My mother made them in Seoul. That's what we lived off during the war. I'll go and sell them in Shin-Okubo.'

'Kkwabaegi? Like the ones you get in the Family Mart? I eat those with Mieko.'

'Aigou!' she spits. 'Much too sugary, those things, the Japanese put sugar in everything!'

'Lotte doughnuts are Korean, aren't they? Mieko's crazy about them.'

'Who's she?'

'You know who she is. The little girl.'

My grandmother says nothing.

'She'd really like to meet you.'

Again, silence.

'Why?'

'I don't know. Just because.'

I glance over at her. She's staring at the railway lines. Her cheeks are flushed. I hear a rumbling sound. The air begins to throb. I grab hold of her as a train thunders past.

It could have been an earthquake. You can't be sure when you hear that sound. I haven't experienced one yet. Not a real one, the kind you feel even in your sleep. I always look around for something to anchor myself to when I hear it. I realise it's futile. When a big earthquake strikes, there's nothing you can do.

'Eh! Don't you worry about me,' my grandmother says. 'I'll still be making doughnuts when I'm old and doddery!'

IT'S AFTER EIGHT when we arrive back at the house. I'm hungry, so is my grandmother. I suggest we make one of her favourites, noodles perhaps; I'll cook. No, she says, we have to wait for my grandfather. We could save him some, I suggest. She shakes her head, says it's sad, eating by yourself. We can have the noodles another time. We'll have leftovers this evening, we can reheat the bento boxes.

She goes out every day to buy them from the stand on the corner. The empty boxes end up in a heap behind the kitchen door, barely rinsed, still covered in grease. I was horrified when I first saw them. I thought back to

the hours we used to spend together cooking, making pancakes, soups and stews: eomuk and soegogi-jin, kimchi and miyeok-guk; and sweet dishes like honey ice cream and hotteok. We'd spend whole afternoons in the kitchen, my grandmother as chef and me as her assistant, her apron knotted around my waist. I was responsible for cleaning up; my grandmother insisted on everything being kept spotless. We bumped into each other constantly in that tiny kitchen. What happened? When did she start buying takeaways?

I'd asked her a while back if she was all right. I was worried about her alone in the house all day. I thought she might be bored. 'I'm fine, I'm fine,' she said, gently stroking my back. 'I take naps.'

And when I asked if she had anything to read, she fired back scathingly, read what? I let it go.

She probably didn't like me drawing attention to the fact that she didn't read. I knew she'd held ambitions to study when she was young, Mathieu had told me. She wanted to become a lawyer. But then the Korean War came and they fled to Japan. And besides, she was a girl, her parents wouldn't have allowed her to go to university.

Trying not to think about how hungry I am, I put the water on to boil and make a jug of black tea. I add some ice cubes to cool it down, stir in some condensed milk. My grandmother turns on the television in the living room. I ask if she wants to play Monopoly. She's thrilled.

We set it up on the low table. My grandmother chooses the wheelbarrow, I take the thimble. It's been twenty years since we last played. I read through the instructions to remind myself of the rules. My grandmother immediately starts installing hotels wherever she lands, whether she owns the property or not. She doesn't like the houses, she says, they're too small.

'That's one of mine,' I say.

She rolls the dice, dislodging the buildings.

'You see,' I say, 'they're righting themselves of their own accord.'

No response. She's too engrossed in the game. She throws a double, moves her wheelbarrow to the 'just visiting' square, throws again. Another double. This time she lands on Lausanne, Rue du Bourg. She buys it. Throws again for the third time.

'Double sixes!' she cries. 'You see! It's my lucky day!'

'Well, no, actually,' I say, after a quick glance at the rules. 'On the third double you have to go to jail.'

'Why? I haven't done anything wrong!'

'That's the game. The rules. It's all the luck of the dice.'

'You're just jealous,' she complains. 'You're cheating.'

I can't show her the proof, the rules are written in French, German and English, languages she doesn't understand. She has a choice between paying to get out or waiting for three goes.

'That's no fun,' she says.

I let her have her way. It would make more sense to play with three people. With my mother. My grandmother says she wants to start the game again. I go to prison in her place. Better to let her play on and keep the game going. I swap our pieces round.

The ice cubes have melted in the jug. Water floats above the milk. I stir it with my spoon. The tea turns cloudy, opaque. I take a sip. It tastes like Mieko's royal milk tea, a little less sweet, perhaps.

When I look up, my grandmother is staring at me.

'Is it my turn?' I ask.

She asks me how I am.

'I'm fine, how are you?' I reply, disconcerted. I say it without thinking. As I would to someone I don't know. It's unsettling.

'I'm fine. What about you?' I say again, more slowly.

'You're tired,' she says. 'You said so earlier, in Shin-Okubo. You work too hard.'

'No, I don't, most of the time I do nothing.'

It's true. Apart from when I'm with Mieko, I spend my days in my room, on the tatami mat, looking up Korea on the internet or playing inane games on my phone. Two weeks have gone by already. And the trip still isn't organised. I'm suddenly seized with panic.

My grandmother has taken the other Monopoly pieces out of the box. The shoe, the iron, the horse and the car. She lines them up along the board.

'You're not enjoying this,' she says.

'Yes, I am.'

'No need to force yourself. You go off and play. I'm fine here, in the living room.'

She nods towards the stairs.

'Okay, okay, go, go.'

'But I'm perfectly happy here with you!'

She looks up, 'Really?'

'Really. Come on. Let's get on with the game.'

I throw the dice, move my piece forward, ignoring the number displayed on the dice. We stare at the board, rolling the dice in turn, lost in our world of Monopoly,

until my grandfather comes home and we clear it all away to set the table for dinner.

LATER IN THE EVENING, I go online, do some searching. September is the best time of year to visit Korea. Ferries go from Fukuoka in southern Japan to Busan. Night crossings are less expensive but they're slow. There are faster ones that only take three hours. We'll book one of those. And then what? Should we stop in Busan for the night to break the journey? Or would it be better to do it all in one day? My grandparents will be tired, but I want to make the most of the time we have there. I google 'port of Busan' and images of bridges pop up. It seems there are several in the bay. The largest is shown from various angles. Ships sail beneath it. An enormous bridge. The

first thing you see when you arrive from Japan by sea. It's visible from a long way off, lit up at night like a bow and arrow aimed at the moon.

Mathieu sends me his news. He's making progress but he has a large group of hikers there, he's very busy. There was a storm last night, with high winds. A couple has arrived with a nine-month-old baby. Seriously. A *baby*! I type a quick answer, not mentioning the baby or Mieko.

There's a message from my mother about my father's latest concert. I still haven't responded to the recording she sent me five days ago. She's probably worried about me but she's afraid to say it. She asks what my grandparents say about her.

Nothing. They don't talk about you.

I read over what I've written. Erase it.

Everything's fine. They send their love.

I close my laptop and roll over onto the floor. Cars throw spray onto the pavement. A child jumps in puddles, his mother pulling him along by the hand, he looks like he's flying.

It's almost twenty years since we last went anywhere together.

My mother, my grandmother and me. In the Museum of Nature and Science in Ueno, the hall devoted to evolution. Images projected onto a circular screen, silhouette figures filing past, men, women and children. On horseback, then in carriages, in cars and finally in a spaceship. They hold hands as they move on, leaping forwards to each new era. The soundtrack reminds me of a song, from the film Noddy in Toyland – four beats to a bar, jaunty. My mother whispers something to my grandmother, they're arguing in Korean, I don't know what about, I hear my mother say the word 'slave' again and again. I wait. I watch the film several times. I want to move on to another room. The next one is full of animals. I ask my mother if I can go and look. She says no, it's time to go home. My grandmother says pointedly that *just for*

once she could let me do as I like, I only want to see a few animals. My mother looks daggers at her.

'Oh, all right,' she says, giving me a push, 'go on then, go on!'

And I go running in to see the exhibition of stuffed animals. My footsteps ring out beneath the vaulted stone ceiling. Bears, tigers, deer, pandas, aboard Noah's ark. Clumps of dried fur fallen on the ground. It's late afternoon. The sky clouds over, daylight fades, the lights come on. I stand in front of the lion and stare into its gaping jaws. The tongue coated in dust. Unseeing eyes. On the walls, huge panels displaying insects, pinned through the belly or the back, legs splayed. I turn round and realise I'm all alone, my mother and grandmother are still in the other room. I run back, bury my face in my mother's skirt, smothering my tears.

'What else did you expect?' she says, speaking in French. 'They're nothing but stuffed animals.' She turns to face my grandmother and adds: 'Old carcasses, with glass beads for eyes.'

Back at the house, my grandmother asked me what my mother had said.

'Nothing,' I lied.

I told them I'd been scared in the museum, imagining the lions would be real. My mother said we could put on a video of *The Lion King* to make me feel better. My grandmother offered to keep me company – she'd never seen a Disney film before. We watched the whole film together, from start to finish.

That was how we started watching cartoons together. After that she'd sometimes put on a video while she was cooking or cleaning. She seemed to understand, even though it was all in French. It was the music she liked, its ubiquitous presence.

My mother cut short our stay that year. My grandfather took us to the airport; my grandmother didn't come, the planes scared her, she said. After that, my mother's visits became more and more scarce; for two years, she sent me to Tokyo by myself for the holidays, and then I started at the lycée and my summers were taken up with activities. When I eventually went back years later, it was Mathieu who came with me.

I WAKE UP at one in the morning to sounds coming from the bathroom. Running water, soft chuckles. I knock on the door. No answer, I go in. My grandmother is leaning over the basin, her shoulders soaked. She wanted to see if the colour would hold, she says. It's all washed away. She titters, and gestures to me to be quiet, my grandfather is asleep upstairs. I help her change her blouse. She carries on chuckling to herself. I dry her hair. She's cold. I rub her skin, soft and papery, dotted with bruises. She's stopped laughing. She stares at her face in the mirror.

'Doddery old fool,' she says.

BY THE TIME we finish our lesson, it's already getting dark. Henriette has asked me to stay on past the usual time, she has a meeting. Mieko declares that she has something to show me. She wants to take me up to the roof.

We climb the emergency staircase and step out onto a platform. Air vents cling to its surface like leeches. Smoke billows up from below. Looking down, all you can see are low-rise buildings, no higher than the lamp-posts, lights coming on in the windows. Signposts. No cars. Everything seems to float, like jellyfish in the sky. Mieko points at the building across the way.

'That's where the bee came from. They're Tokyo bees. They make cherry blossom honey because cherry blossoms are the only flowers in the city.'

It takes me a while to make out the hives. Little houses lined up by the dozen on the roof.

'I'm cold, I'm going to get something warm,' Mieko says, heading back inside.

I walk over to the edge. Cawing of crows. Ambulance sirens. Muffled sounds. A spider spins its web on the railing; it looks as big as the rooftop baseball pitches in the distance, their safety nets.

A player, his hand frozen in mid-air, waiting to catch a ball. He hurls his body forward in slow motion, surely it will take him years to return to his original position. I stand watching this lone player for a moment, mirroring his gestures, their infinite slowness, wondering if he really is playing or if it's a trick of perception, if time has stalled and slowed down all movement.

'Onni?'

Mieko is staring at me, holding a thermos and two towels. I become conscious of the way I'm standing: on one foot, one leg raised with bent knee, one hand in the air. I adjust my stance, show too much enthusiasm for the thermos, say it's a sure sign that summer is ending.

'It's cold,' she laughs. 'It's royal milk tea.'

We wrap ourselves in the towels. They're too short for me, they stop just below my stomach.

'The bees are dying,' says Mieko. 'So are the trees. There aren't nearly as many as there used to be in the city. One day they'll all be dead, and then we'll all die too.'

I turn to look at her.

'I'm scared too, you know.'

'Of the bees?'

'Of the trees dying. Everything. That's why I like going up high in the mountains, at least it's normal for there to be no trees there.'

'I've never seen anything like that,' says Mieko.

'Maybe you will some day.'

We huddle together, drink the tea straight from the thermos, passing it back and forth between us. The crescent moon has come into view, lying on its side. It always surprises me in Japan, the way the moon seems to be sleeping, while in Switzerland it stands upright. I tell Mieko. She cranes her neck to look at the moon from a different angle.

'Are you looking forward to going away?' I ask.

'Mum says it's for my future.'

'What about you? What do you think?'

'I don't know really. It's ages away. When are we going to the pachinko parlour?'

'I'm not sure there'll be enough time,' I mumble.

'Later – when the holidays are over!'

I say we'll have to see. Her chin puckers. I'm afraid she might start to cry, so I say light-heartedly:

'When I was little, I wanted to be a chlorophyll splitter.'

She looks at me quizzically. I explain to her what chlorophyll is, that it helps plants to breathe, like our blood helps us. Blood and chlorophyll are actually very similar, four atoms grouped around a central atom. The only difference is that chlorophyll has magnesium where haemoglobin has iron.

'I used to think that if humans could work out how to break chlorophyll down, extract the magnesium and insert it into our bloodstream, we'd be able to produce our own oxygen simply by exposing ourselves to light. I decided it could be a job, being a chlorophyll splitter. That's what I wanted to do when I grew up.'

'Why didn't you?'

'I started thinking about splitting atoms and about that being a way of making atomic bombs.'

Mieko is quiet for a few minutes, thinking.

'How old are you, actually?'

'Thirty. Well, almost.'

'Thirty! I'm ten.'

'I know,' I say, irritated.

'When's your birthday?'

'Soon.'

'Soon when?'

'20th of August.'

She counts on her fingers, overjoyed suddenly, I've no idea why.

The baseball player has gone. The deserted pitch is bathed in radiance beneath the lights. Artificial daylight. The wind picks up. Tokyo's stations come into view, criss-crossed with lines, some overhead, some at ground level, trains running along them.

'The trains look like fish, don't they?' Mieko says.

'Sort of. Some of them.'

'Did you know that a long, long time ago, oceans covered the whole of the planet? Fish could swim anywhere, even above this building. That's why my father wanted his trains to look like fish. Or dragons. Dragons evolved from fish.'

She laughs. 'And there are slug trains too – trams, and the metro, underground worms. But they're not my

dad's trains.'

The Shinkansen is the fastest train in the world, I say, she can be proud of her father for making it possible for so many people to travel so far so fast. She hates her father, she says, he only worked on building those trains so he could run away from her and her mother. She stands, folds up our towels, her movements uncharacteristically harsh.

'I'm hungry,' she declares. 'Let's go back down.'

She wants an omelette. The fridge is full of eggs, her mother has stocked up: quails' eggs, hens' eggs, scrambled eggs, square omelettes from Family Mart, egg salads. There's even a vacuum-packed fried egg, its yolk bulbous beneath the transparent packaging. I take out one of the omelettes. Mieko shakes her head, she wants to make it from scratch.

'Are you sure?'

Making an omelette wasn't included in Henriette's instructions, I say.

'Yes, it was,' she says, cracking an egg on the side of the pan.

I watch nervously. Egg white runs down along the

shell and over her fingers, like drool from a sleeper's lips. I haven't handled raw eggs since I came upon one with an embryo. I fiddle with the ready-made omelette, feeling its texture through the packaging. Like a sponge. I give it a squeeze and something yellowish oozes from it. I let go and it's sucked back in. Mieko lights the burner, she's beaten at least ten eggs.

'Mum says I have to eat food from abroad so I can get used to it before I leave. Apparently I'll be ready to go when all my cells have regenerated with new kinds of food.'

I ask her if she knows why her mother wants me to call her Henriette, I'm sure it's not her real name. She shrugs.

'Probably because of Heidi.'

'Heidi?'

'It starts with the same letter.'

The eggs start to sputter in the pan, exploding limply, shooting specks of yellow in every direction.

Mieko presses her finger to one, puts it in her mouth:

'Mmmm, that's good, nice and crisp.'

After we've eaten, she asks me to help her in the shower.

She undresses, throws her clothes in a ball into the basin. The bathroom is too small for two people. I sit on the toilet and stare discreetly at the floor. I haven't seen a female child's body since I grew up myself. The heat is intense, but Mieko still turns the hot water on full. Steam envelops us. I look over at her. She's rubbing herself with a facecloth. Smooth skin, arms so skinny you want to grip them firmly to stop them falling off. Angular shoulder blades, pointed, like fins. The soap refuses to lather. I think of Henriette's dry skin, tell myself they need something more moisturising, less harsh. When she closes her eyes to wash her face, I take a good look at her. She hasn't started to develop yet. Just two nipples, scarcely defined, two drops of water on paper. Maybe she won't need to wear a bra, any more than her mother does.

I was only a year older than she is now when my breasts began to develop. When my grandmother noticed, she pressed her thumbs against my chest, as if to push the swelling back inside me, as if it didn't belong there. My mother had bought me a bra just before the holidays. It was too tight, it cut into my flesh, I was ashamed of it. I'd hide in the toilets, rubbing my breasts, fretting about the lack of a lock on the door, terrified my grandmother

would walk in without knocking.

The humidity in the bathroom is becoming unbearable. My hair is glued to my temples. I brush it aside, flap my skirt around my thighs. Mieko is still soaping herself. I go and wait in the living room.

I browse the bookshelves. My eye falls on a French translation of Heidi, between two classic Pléiade volumes. The pages are dotted with notes in Japanese, in green pen, like blades of grass left to dry between the pages. It's hard to read the text beneath the green. Lines stand out.

The eagle looks down on the villagers from the sky:

'If you would separate and each go your own way and come up here and live on a height as I do, it would be better for you!'

Or the goatherd's grandmother talking to Heidi: 'The house is going to pieces, and in the night, when the two others are asleep, I often lie awake in fear and trembling, thinking that the whole place will give way and fall and kill us. And there is not a creature to mend anything for us, for Peter does not understand such work.'

Feeling uncomfortable, I put the book back on the shelf. A leaflet falls out from the back cover. Heidi's Village. I open it out. A theme park, based on the Ghibli studios' animated version. Located in the prefecture of Yamanashi, near the Hokuto hills, two hours from Tokyo. I place the leaflet on the coffee table, linger over the shelf of children's picture books. Geometric shapes, bright coloured squares and rectangles. Titles I don't recognise, except for Ernest & Célestine. I'm sure I've read this one too, I think, as I open the book.

Watercolours. Beige wash. Ernest seems smaller than I remember him being. And little Célestine seems much bigger. They're in the forest, putting up a tent, a homeless person comes to live in it. I'm startled to see how few words there are to a page. It seemed so long when my mother read it to me, there were so many words: Célestine going to school, reading books, stories within stories, Ernest falling in love with a polar bear he meets in the frozen north. There's nothing of that here, either in the words or the pictures. Did my mother make it all up? I remember asking her to speak slowly, making sure what she said matched the words on the page. But

I hadn't learnt to read then, and when I did start reading by myself I'd lost interest in Ernest and Célestine.

The end, already. The homeless person moves out, leaving presents for his mystery hosts. I close the book.

A bear and a baby mouse. An odd pairing for a story. Célestine must have been an orphan, I suppose, her mother eaten by a cat. Now that I think about it, Ernest's broad, vaulted back speaks of a burden of suffering from long ago, from the time when he comforted Célestine, took her in. I'd never thought of it like that before.

Hearing the slip-slap of wet feet, I look up. Wrapped in her mother's robe, Mieko sits down beside me. She points at the Heidi's Village leaflet.

'I went there on a school trip. It's rubbish.'

'I wouldn't mind going there.'

'I'm warning you, it's for little kids.'

She takes a deep breath, exhales jerkily.

'Do you have trouble breathing? I often see you doing that with your mouth.'

She shakes her head, says she's fine. Then, nodding

towards *Ernest & Célestine*, 'Will you read it to me?'

I start at the beginning, but she flips to a page near the middle. 'I like this bit best.'

We turn off the lights, except for one on the wall next to the sofa. As I read, Mieko slumps against me, I can feel her getting heavier. She falls asleep, her head in my lap. Henriette comes home and finds us in the same position. I haven't moved, not wanting to wake Mieko. When I get up to leave, she waves her hand, like Célestine in the beam of a torch, waving to Ernest from the tent.

THE NEXT DAY Henriette messages me. Mieko wants me to take her to Heidi's Village. She suggests we go on the 20th. We could celebrate my birthday at their place when we get back. They'll be away until then, spending a week at a seaside resort in Okinawa. The tone of her message is cool. I feel somewhat wounded that neither of them has mentioned this beach holiday to me. I didn't say anything to Henriette about it being my birthday. Mieko must have told her. I wasn't planning anything special for the day, I haven't even talked to my grandparents about it. As far as they're concerned, I've already turned thirty: in the Korean system, a person's age is counted

from the moment of conception. I reread the message, say yes to the invitation.

With Mieko away, I feel at a loss. I spend too much time in my bedroom, crushed by the heat. I'd like to go out to a museum, leave the neighbourhood, but my grandmother worries so much when I go out. I hear her humming a lullaby in Korean, always the same one. It's nothing like the ones she used to sing to me when I was little, I don't recognise it. Sometimes I go and wander in the cemetery, listen to the cicadas shrieking. I walk along the quiet street that runs behind the station, sit on the stairs sipping ice-cold amazake, surrounded by cats. This must be the meeting-ground for all the cats in the neighbourhood.

We're supposed to be leaving in two weeks and my grand-father still hasn't confirmed the dates for our trip. I don't dare ask him again. There's so much to organise. I start by searching online to get as much information as I can about the trains. We'd need to take the Shinkansen and go up the east side via Kyoto and Hiroshima. Five hours in all, a long journey for two elderly people. We could stop

over at the island of Miyajima, where Mieko went with her father. It's only a few kilometres from Hiroshima.

I mention it to my grandparents. It's up to me, they say, they're happy to go along with whatever I decide. They're not really listening, they're too busy staring at the television.

Once in a while, I play Monopoly with my grandmother. We're just starting our game one day when she nods towards my bedroom and says, out of the blue: 'Okay, okay, go, go.'

I feign protest, carry on playing. After a while, I stand up and go downstairs, feeling sad but relieved.

I can hear them talking upstairs; snippets of conversation float down to me through the ceiling. My grandfather, holding forth about the Shiny. More and more women are playing these days but they don't really feel welcome. They're mostly non-smokers. Some parlours have separate sections for smokers nowadays. Some of them target women players, provide childcare. Perhaps it was time to make some changes at the Shiny.

I tense up when I hear this. They never mention Korea. I write to Mathieu: the time for our trip is fast approaching, I feel as if I'm dragging them there. Nothing seems to be happening here. I'm starting to think we'll never get there. He tells me to see it from their perspective, they must be feeling anxious, everything will have changed, it's been such a long time since they left their home. Do I need any help? He can buy the tickets, do some of the translating for me. No, it's all fine, I reply, feeling some-what piqued. I can take care of it. Everything is fine. On his side, the thesis is coming together. He can see the end in sight. He wishes me a happy birthday, he won't be able to write to me on the day but he'll make it up to me when I get back, promise.

I have a craving for marzipan. Fatty, comforting. My mother used to give it to me to drink, watered down. She fed it to me in a bottle, even though I was much too big by then for a bottle.

I've broken my record at Tetris. I've been stuck on level fifteen for days.

The days are beginning to draw in. The sky is dark by seven in the evening. I lie on the floor and gaze out of the window. Women's calves, men's shoes, heels trodden down by the weight of bodies borne for too long. Salarymen, I can tell from the rigid gait, the uniform. Footsteps of people in a hurry, people dragging their feet. I turn away, try to block them out, but then I see their shadows file past on my bedroom wall, distorted, magnified in the beam of the streetlight. Sometimes a taxi parks in front of the window, the driver asleep, forehead resting on the steering wheel.

I go to the Family Mart to buy some shampoo, select one with almond milk, my favourite, highly moisturising. At the edge of my vision, I catch a glimpse of my grandfather through the door at the back, inside the Shiny. He walks slowly down the aisle, stopping in front of every machine to give it a slap on the side, as if he were urging on a beast of burden at the end of a long day's labour. He goes back to the desk, takes his seat beside the security guard. A player comes up and hands in his collection of balls, walks out holding a stuffed bear.

I step out of the shop into a downpour. Warm rain falling in a steady stream, washing away the film of grease from every surface. A summer storm, short-lived. I decide to wait it out.

I walk up to the sandwich-board woman, stand behind her under the awning. She has a patch of bare skin where her hair is swept to one side in a plait. Water splashes from the canopy. Drops land on the back of her neck. She doesn't flinch. The rigid cardboard panels hang down to her ankles, slapping against her body, buffeted by the wind. I take another step towards her, she smells of rain and laundry soap. I can't see her face. Her eyelids are cast down beneath the peaked cap, her shoulders hunched. Passers-by take no notice of us. They walk on. Some stop in the doorway of the Shiny. I adjust my position, try to see their faces – I only ever see their legs from my bedroom window. Their heads are turned away, their collars turned up, hands deep in their pockets. I step out onto the pavement, in front of the sand-wich-board woman. In an instant, I'm soaked through. My clothes feel heavy, like a suit of armour. People step carefully around me, avoiding all contact. Behind me, the sandwich-board girl goes on chanting her ditty into the microphone. I have an urge to walk right up to her, rip away the boards and shout in her face: look at me.

THE HEATWAVE INTENSIFIES. On the morning of my birthday, the weather presenter issues a warning, urging the populace, especially the elderly, to avoid going out, to stay inside in the cool and drink plenty of fluids.

'Did you hear that?' I call out to my grandmother as I tie my shoelaces.

I've prepared bottles of water for her to drink during the day. I can hear her moving about upstairs. She seems strangely agitated. I sensed it last night. She keeps going in and out of the kitchen, walking round in circles. Since breakfast this morning, I've had the feeling she's waiting for me to leave.

'Okay, okay, go, go!' she shouts back at me from the living room.

I meet Mieko in Shinagawa. We take the Yamanote line to Shinjuku together, where the trains for the Yamanashi Prefecture leave from.

'How was it with your mum? Everything all right?'

She nods, staring out of the window. She's hardly said a word all morning. When I finally ask her why she's so quiet she says it's because the holidays are almost over.

We leave behind the outskirts of Tokyo, emerging into countryside. Mossy forests. Small valleys. One hour later, at the end of the Chuo line, we take a bus, together with a handful of old men, all wearing bandanas. The bus jolts along a gravel road for about ten kilometres, dropping us beside a high wall that marks the perimeter of Heidi's Village.

For some reason, entry into the park is free of charge today. There's no one at the reception desk. On the other

side of the wall, we emerge onto a square surrounded by medieval façades that are vaguely Alsatian in style. A church, a town hall, a restaurant, a museum dedicated to the animated film of Heidi, and a tower boasting a panoramic view. A sign in gothic-style lettering on the façade of the town hall: 'Zürich'. Except for the old people, who've disappeared up the stairs between the tower and the church, Mieko and I are the only ones here. We climb the stairs. They lead to a miniature train station, the platform lined with a single long bench. The rails disappear into an area of dense greenery, criss-crossed with walkways. The bell tower strikes eleven. There's a smell of cut grass.

'Can't we walk?' I ask Mieko, who's already sitting down.

'No. But there's the train. It's coming now,' she says, pointing towards the far side of the park.

Shielding my eyes with my hand I can just make out a red train carriage winding its way through a field of sunflowers. Around it, old men are at work, harvesting, watering, clearing the ground.

Piped music fills the air. Familiar-sounding. 'Edelweiss' from The Sound of Music. Mieko cranes forward, gazing intently at the pond on the other side of the track.

'Look at that grey fish, the one with white spots. It's a cleaner fish. Did you know they keep on getting bigger, for the whole of their lives?'

'I know. I had one in my fish tank when I was little.'

'They can't grow up properly when they're in an aquarium. They don't live as long, they die when they're still no bigger than babies.'

I tip my chin in acknowledgement. That wasn't the reason my fish died. I was thirteen, just starting at middle school. For some reason I'd become obsessed with having an aquarium. My parents were sceptical at first but in the end, they bought me a thirty-litre tank, with a pair of guppies, four neon tetras and a pleco. The salesperson said the pleco would clean up all the algae and other impurities in the tank. It didn't quite work out that way. The algae spread all over the tank and before long it obscured everything. I despaired as I watched the fish die one by one, all except the pleco. I thought it was probably very happy to have so much food all to itself. But the pleco died too and after that we grew cacti. I found out later that I'd been misinformed. Plecos need more than algae in their diet. I should have given it special food, just like the other fish, with specially adapted nutrients.

The train pulls in, two old men get off, we climb in. We're off, the pace so slow it'd be quicker to walk. The driver, in his peaked cap, stares straight ahead. We've barely travelled a hundred metres when he applies the brakes and calls out: 'Fifteen-minute halt.'

The attraction we're visiting is a log cabin, Heidi's grandfather's. A chain slung across the open door bars visitors from entering. We stand in front of the display, a single room with a wooden table on which pieces of artificial food are arranged, with labels written in Japanese: 'cheese', 'meat', 'bread'. A ladder leads up to the loft where Heidi sleeps.

Mieko examines the exhibits carefully, putting on a show of attention for her guest who is seeing it for the first time. I look around the cabin. Cut-out rabbits stand on the bare earth at the back, holding up a placard, warped by sunlight. 'Sorry, we are absent due to maintenance' it reads, in English. I feel a migraine coming on. I'm only too glad to get back on the train and find some shade even though the heat is even more intense under the metal roof of the carriage.

Meanwhile, the village square has come to life. In the restaurant, women fuss over a fondue pot, their

movements visible through the orange-tinted steam. Mieko and I sit down on the steps of the church. With a bloom of sweat on her she looks like a doll, brand new, still wrapped in plastic. She turns to face me, asks for my permission to go back to the garden.

'Yes, you can go.'

She walks with heavy steps towards the stairs. I lean back against the wall of the church and feel it shudder. I peer through a stained-glass window and realise it's only a façade, made of plaster, supported by a metal frame.

I do a tour of the shop. On offer are figurines, cows made of wood with red or black spots. They remind me of my first school trip, to a farm in Appenzell. I must have been seven or eight at the time. The farmer's wife made little cows just like these. At the end of the visit we were all given some strong-smelling cheese. Most of my classmates threw it away, especially the girls, who put on extravagant displays of disgust for the benefit of the boys. I hid mine in my bag. I wanted to take it home for my mother. In the bus, the smell started to waft out. Everyone turned in my direction and someone said I stank and told me to go and sit somewhere else. I moved

to the back of the bus, hugging my bag close in an effort to contain the smell. By the time I reached home, fat had seeped out onto my homework notebook. It smelt of cheese for the rest of the year. But my gift was a success. My mother loved it.

It seems a long time since Mieko went off by herself. I walk back through the park and catch sight of her squatting on her heels beside the pond. The horizon shimmers in the heat. I don't want to disturb her. I wander among the flower beds, keep walking to where the vegetation is denser, not so well maintained, until I come to a greenhouse, as big as the grandfather's chalet, in the shadow of a windmill. On the metal door is an inscription in Japanese lettering, the characters interwoven with kittens: 'Clara's Sanatorium'. I go inside, amused.

The air feels cooler in the greenhouse. Gardening tools, a collection of miniature olive trees growing in containers. Water burbles from an imitation marble fountain. I taste olive oil on my tongue, full and round, the taste of summer holidays. A plastic duck paddles on the spot, its

beak caught in the spigot. A caterpillar crawls along the edge. Feeling suddenly dizzy, I lean against the fountain, almost crushing the caterpillar.

'Are you all right?'

A woman is watching me from the back of the greenhouse, a tray of olives in one hand, a pair of secateurs in the other. Immaculate uniform, in the park's colours: red and white, a curious hybrid of the Swiss and Japanese flags. She brings me a glass of water from the drinking fountain.

'You need fluids in this heat. You'll get heatstroke. Are you from here?' she asks as she wipes her hands.

I tell her I'm Korean.

'Oh,' she says, smiling. 'You speak very good Japanese.'

Her teeth look discoloured, like shrivelled olives, her mouth must be dry.

'What I meant was, are you new here? Are you on the staff?'

'No, I live in Switzerland.'

She blinks.

'Oh well, in that case,' she says, smiling again, relaxed, 'I'm so sorry, but you can't stay here. It says so there, on the door.'

'I'm sorry, I didn't see.'

As I'm leaving, she adds, with concern in her voice, 'You really don't look too well. You should go home.'

Mieko is sitting in front of the church, waiting for me. In her lap, an empty sandwich wrapper and an unopened can of Pocari Sweat. She hands it to me and I open it and take a swig. Warm, slightly salty. I set it down between us.

Mieko points to it timidly, 'Dare I?' she asks me in French.

I hand it to her immediately, ashamed not to have realised that she was waiting for me to drink first. I hadn't stopped to think about whether she was hungry or thirsty. I ought to explain to her that she's used the wrong verb to ask me. It's too late now. Secretly, I find it reassuring that she makes mistakes. It reminds me that she is only a child.

In the bus on the way back, Mieko holds my hand. Suddenly, she pulls away from me and sticks her mouth against the window, making loud sucking sounds.

'Hey! What are you doing?'

She pulls her lips away for a moment.

'Cleaner fish.'

She takes a deep breath, ready to start again. I put my hand on her shoulder to restrain her.

'Don't do that! It's filthy!'

She slumps back in her seat, obediently. Her lips have left a mark on the window, a circle of saliva, chilled by the air conditioning. I close my eyes to avoid catching the other passengers' gaze. A few minutes later I feel the weight of her head on my shoulder. She looks as though she's sleeping but she whispers, her voice thick with sleep, 'I'm so glad you're coming back again this evening.'

I LET MIEKO get off at Shinagawa. I'll be there in a little while, I tell her, I need to go back and freshen up at my grandparents' house, change clothes. And to get the shampoo I bought for Mieko, I think to myself, I forgot it this morning, I left it in my room.

I think I have a temperature.

Back in Nippori, I glance automatically through the window of the Shiny. No sign of my grandfather. He must be down in the basement, in the storage area. I cross the street. The house is dark. At this time of day?

Something must be wrong. With a growing sense of foreboding, I call out to my grandmother from the hallway. No response. The light switch in the entrance hall isn't working. I feel my way up the stairs to the living room and turn on the light.

Playmobil figures stand dotted about the room, their hands raised in applause. Their gaze is turned towards the table set with our three bowls, a platter of iced noodles in the centre, topped with the Bambi figurine. My grandparents are seated cross-legged on their cushions, my grandfather wearing a pointy cardboard hat.

'We've made you noodles for long life!' my grandmother announces.

Noodles, long ones, a Korean birthday tradition.

'I bought you some beer, and your grandfather boiled the water for the noodles!'

My grandfather elbows her, she's already said too much.

'You should've let me know . . .' I mutter, caught off guard.

They gaze blankly at me. I mumble something about not being able to stay, that I have to go out, I'm going to be late, regretting every word as soon as I utter it.

'But you've been out all day,' my grandmother says. 'You've only just got home.'

I try and explain: Mieko and Henriette's invitation, I'd have said no, if only I'd known. She cuts me off. I hadn't told them my plans either. I never tell them anything. She's even bought a chocolate cake. And as if to emphasise the point, she goes into the kitchen and comes back with a cake, iced and decorated with the number thirty.

It's not my fault, I think to myself, if I don't tell them anything. If I can't speak to them in Korean. I can't help it if I live in Switzerland and speak French. I studied Japanese for their sakes. Because this is where they live and that's what people speak here.

'Tomorrow?' I mouth.

'Tomorrow it won't be your birthday any more.'

'Let's have it now, then.'

I sit down opposite my grandfather. He's been staring at the noodles ever since I came in. I fill up our bowls. My grandmother is still standing, the cake in her hands.

'Please sit,' I say.

'You don't love me any more,' she declares stubbornly.

'Aigou . . .' my grandfather sighs, his eyes still fixed on the noodles. 'Don't be childish. Come along now.'

She sets the cake down on the ground, faces my grandfather and says:

'What do you know about anything? You're oblivious to everything.' And pointing at me, she adds: 'Do you even know what she does all day long?'

My grandfather flinches, cowering almost.

She carries on. 'She says she's come here for our sakes, but she's never here. She's out all the time.'

'That's not true,' I say, defending myself, 'I've only seen Mieko four times.'

It is strange though, I feel I've known this child for a long time, that somehow I know her really well.

'And what's more,' I add, 'she said she wanted to meet you. I'd have liked to bring her back here with me.'

'So why didn't you?' my grandmother asks, suddenly very calm.

I look at her, baffled. On the platform at Shin-Okubo, when I'd mentioned the possibility of her meeting Mieko, she'd said no, hadn't she? Or did she? I'd convinced myself she'd said no. Now I'm not so sure. One way or the other, I can see now that it's me that doesn't want them to meet. The two of them speaking Japanese together. I wouldn't be able to stand it, my grandmother telling Mieko her life story, just as she did with Mathieu. And me shut out again, unable to join in their conversation.

'If you'd rather,' I say flatly, 'I could be your sandwich-board woman.'

My grandmother is tucking into the icing on the cake. The number thirty comes off in chunks, the cake is starting to look like a field of muddy snow. Her hands shake. My grandfather tips his chin to indicate that I can leave, that he'll deal with her. I go down to the hall, on the verge of tears. Outside, the wind has picked up. Orange sky, streaked with lightning. A storm, but no rain. I have no desire to celebrate this birthday, even less to go out. I'm sweating. I'd like to sleep.

From upstairs I hear my grandmother's voice: 'Have they at least made you some noodles?' she rasps.

As I close the door behind me, I hear her saying to my grandfather that it's his fault, it's all his fault, he dragged her to Japan, he let my mother leave, and now he's driving me away.

I make my escape, as fast as I can.

HENRIETTE AND MIEKO have dressed up for the occasion. Mieko is wearing a salmon-pink dress, Henriette a taupe-grey silk blouse. I've barely come in the door when Mieko announces that she has a present for me and goes down to her room to fetch it. Henriette pours me a glass of umeshu and starts preparing the salad. She hasn't caught the sun as Mieko has, but her skin seems even drier than before. When she bends, her vertebrae protrude beneath her blouse. While Mieko is out of the room, I thank her for inviting me.

'It was Mieko's idea,' she says.

'I might have guessed.'

She raises an eyebrow slightly. I can't muster the energy to make amends for my lack of tact. Luckily Mieko comes back. She hands me an oblong package tied at either end, like an outsize bonbon. She wants me to open it straight away. I unwrap the gift.

Two dolls made of bamboo sticks, with golf balls for heads, painted green and stuck on with Sellotape. Scraps of dried seaweed glued on for hair. It still smells of the sea.

'You and me, in green,' she explains.

She stares at my face to see my reaction.

'What did I tell you about the seaweed?' Henriette says.

'But it's to help them breathe. With chlorophyll.'

'I think they're lovely,' I mumble.

'They're kokeshi dolls,' Henriette explains. 'People used to make them to remember the babies they killed because they couldn't feed them. Mieko knows perfectly well. I'm very sorry.'

She sets the utensils on the table while I rewrap the dolls with exaggerated delicacy as Mieko looks on, head down, completely still.

Six crabs, arranged in a circle on a platter, a cup of white sauce in the centre. The platter takes up most of the table. Henriette uses a mallet to crack the crabs, striking them on the legs and the body. She hands us the claws, pieces of the shell still clinging to them. I enquire about their holidays. Their answers are polite but uninformative. I tell them how I spent mine. Walks behind the cemetery in Nippori, the lounging cats, the taste of the rice drink made by the Indian couple in the traditional shopping street. I talk for a while and eventually grind to a halt.

'What's this?' Mieko asks, extracting a piece of transparent filament from a crab. She grimaces.

'It looks like moult,' I say, 'old skin.'

And then again, enunciating clearly for Henriette's benefit: 'Moult.'

'Moult,' Mieko repeats, wrapping the piece of crab in her napkin. 'I'll keep it.'

'No, don't. It'll go off.'

I take it out of her hand and put it on my plate, while Henriette looks on in astonishment. I'm annoyed with myself for teaching Mieko this word, she won't forget it.

I go back to my food. The meal continues in silence. Outside, the wind moans. I fumble with the crab. Henriette passes me yet another claw. I shake my head.

'You don't like it?'

'I do, but I've had enough.'

Mieko pushes her plate away.

'Me too,' she says.

Henriette looks at her daughter, then at me: 'I don't like it either. None of us likes crab.'

She throws the claw back onto the platter. It lands with a splash. Henriette pays no attention.

'Off you go,' she says, with a tilt of her chin. 'Go and play.'

We go downstairs to the swimming pool. I open my bag, take out the shampoo and place it on the desk. Mieko stretches out on the bed in her usual position, prone with her head in the pillow.

'It's not your fault,' she says, her voice muffled.

'What's not my fault?'

'Mum being sad. It was Dad who liked to eat crab.'

She says she'd like to hear my dad playing the organ. I don't have my laptop with me. And anyway, I reflect, the only recording I have is the one my mother sent me, of him playing 'Happy Birthday'.

'But he's your dad!' she says accusingly, turning round to face me.

'Next time.'

'You always say that. And then we never do it. Like seeing your grandmother. Or the pachinko parlour.'

'We went to Disneyland, didn't we? And to Heidi's Village.'

I try and explain to her that my grandmother is an old woman. She's eight times as old as Mieko. She's tired. Surely Mieko can understand that?

'And what is it about pachinko?' I ask her. 'It's nothing but a tacky machine, a heap of plastic and old metal!'

Mieko doesn't respond. After a while, she says that the balls that spurt out of the machines make her think of fish eggs. Like tadpoles with no tails. She lowers her head. She'd like to touch them, see what they feel like. I stifle a nervous laugh. She's lying with her forehead jammed against the side of the pool, eyes closed. The holidays are almost over. She doesn't want to go back to school.

I sit down beside her, do what I can to reassure her, she doesn't need to worry, she's a bright kid. She turns her head towards me and I bend down and plant a kiss on her forehead. She pulls away and I sit upright, embarrassed. Of course. How could I forget? People don't kiss in Japan. I'd acted spontaneously.

'I can't stay,' I tell her, getting up to leave. 'But I'll come back. Soon.'

'Do you think he's dead?' she says quietly as I close the door.

I freeze. She can't see me from where she is.

'I'd prefer it if he was,' she says. 'At least I'd know where he was.'

I can tell from the rustling of sheets that she's climbed under the covers. I close the door without a sound.

Henriette is still at the table, a strong smell of seafood filling the room. She's shelling crabs, piling the flesh onto a plate, sucking at the claws, drawing out the juice. She stops when she sees me. She looks down at the crabmeat:

'They'd go off otherwise.'

I nod in acknowledgement and leave.

I glance back at her from the hallway. Her back is turned, her shoulders shaking, arms pinned to her sides as she sobs in silence.

I COME DOWN with a fever. An ear infection. I try and call Henriette to let her know. She doesn't pick up, I leave a voice message.

My grandmother makes me rice porridge, watches me eat it, sighing plaintively.

'Aigou, yeppun seki . . . Poor baby, pretty little thing.'

I turn away, repulsed by the word *seki*, a term usually applied to young animals. It makes me feel like a calf. I hear her creeping down the stairs, trying not to make a sound, opening the door a crack. She thinks I'm sleeping. If I stir, she shuts the door with a start. Sometimes she comes in, strokes my face, feels my

forehead, my cheeks, touches my nose. Her fingers feel like flies crawling on me but I don't resist. I can't muster the energy. She opens the window to let in some fresh air, wants to give me medicine, caramel, stuff me full of honey. I'm worried that she doesn't know what she's doing. If only my mother were here, she'd know what to do. So would Mathieu.

My head throbs. The smallest of sounds is painful. My grandparents' footsteps on the ceiling above me, the rumbling of car engines, the click of heels on the side-walk. The pachinko girl. Her voice. Piercing. Repetitive. Stopping me from sleeping. I want to seize the boards, crush them against her chest, arrest the flow of words. I hear my grandmother telling my grandfather it's his fault I'm ill. I hate to hear them arguing. It scares me.

One evening, I go upstairs and find my grandfather asleep on the sofa, mouth open, teeth bared, hanging by a thread to receded gums.

The infection doesn't clear. My grandfather calls the doctor, who prescribes an antibiotic. Blood pounds in my head, all other sensations recede. After dinner, I sit between my grandparents, watching television, unable to hear. The news comes on, images of an earthquake. Aftershocks from last year's perhaps.

At night, my anxiety increases. I pull the covers up to my chin, in spite of the heat. If I need to get up to go to the toilet, I wait until I can't hold on any longer. I force myself to stay awake, believing that nothing will change, nothing will age, so long as I'm not asleep. I feel trapped, the ground beneath me is poisoned, the earth's crust itself as toxic as the liquid oozing from my ears.

LITTLE BY LITTLE, my hearing comes back. I don't realise it at first; I still hear only silence in the space that should be filled by the sandwich-board girl's lament. Not until I leave the house, my brain still foggy from the infection, do I realise she's not there. My grandfather has let her go. He's removed the loudspeaker too.

'She wasn't very good,' he says by way of explanation. 'And we're going away soon, aren't we?'

He asks me for the dates of our trip, wants to know if I've already bought the tickets.

It's happening, I write to Mathieu excitedly, it's happening, we're going. In ten days.

I ask my mother to send me some clips of my father playing the organ. Mieko starts school in a week. I'll go over and see her before we leave for Korea.

I'm sleeping better. It's suddenly much cooler, the temperature is back down to normal for early September.

I haven't heard from Henriette. I spend my days tidying the house. Vacuuming. Dusting. I've cleaned out the fridge, put the kimchi in the bin, washed the empty bento boxes, disinfected everything. I sort through my mother's things in my bedroom, untangle the wires of the extension cords, throw out clothes that no one will ever wear again. Mieko's dolls have lost their hair. I decide to discard the bamboo parts but keep the heads. I rinse them off and put them in with my clothes to take back to Geneva with me. I find some boards marked out in squares stashed away in a box, old Korean games, an

assortment of pebbles and sticks. I pack them up. Maybe we'll play them in the train, my grandparents will be able to teach me.

My grandmother sits in the living room surrounded by her Playmobil pieces, watching me work. She doesn't understand why I'm doing so much tidying and organising, we're only going for a few days. I explain to her that when you come back from a trip, it's nice to find your house clean and tidy.

'Yes, you're right,' she exclaims delightedly. 'Aigou! What would I do without you?'

The bathroom is more of a challenge. I try organising at first, then decide to throw everything away: wipes, dried-up nail polish, cotton wool pads, mouldy creams that have started to resemble cottage cheese.

One evening, my grandmother tries to pull out the Playmobil children's hair using a pair of scissors. When her attempts at cutting fail, she stabs at them with the points of the blades.

'You're bleeding!' I say as I walk by.

She stares at me in surprise.

'There, on your chin. Didn't you feel anything?'

'No.'

'It didn't hurt?'

She has a cut running all the way down her chin. I clean it, relieved to see it's only a superficial wound. My grandmother fusses over the dressing. No. She didn't feel anything. Nothing at all. She picks up the Playmobil boy, rubs his head sheepishly, throws it back on the pile. I pick up the scissors to see if I can do any better. The plastic is surprisingly tough.

'See,' she says, 'old people aren't the only ones to be goofy. You never take me seriously, do you?'

Gradually, she too is overcome with the need to be busy organising. She makes piles of clothes, stuffs them into suitcases, for herself and for my grandfather. Now I'm the one pointing out to her that we're only going for a week: it's still warm, there's no point in taking so many clothes. She gets annoyed, says she knows what she's doing, I don't know what I'm talking about, it can be very cold in Korea, the weather can change from one day to the next, all of a sudden it can feel like Siberia.

Sometimes she freezes, gazes at the suitcases, the bags of rubbish piled up in the hallway. She looks at me, stunned. She starts pulling out the things I've put aside to throw away, says we have to keep them, the papers, creams, cotton wool pads, they're hers, I have no right to put my paws all over them. She makes fists, aims at my back, as if she's going to hit me. Then she changes her mind and puts everything back where it was. I'm right, she says, it's time to throw these things out.

My mother hasn't replied to my request for recordings of my father. She's usually so quick to respond. And then one morning, a package from my mother arrives in the post. There's a letter inside. She's sorry it took so long, the files were too big to upload, they've saved them on CDs.

'What's that?' my grandmother asks looking over my shoulder.

'From Papa. For Mieko.'

I turn on the CD player in the living room. My father has really gone all out. There are four CDs. Everything from requiem masses to film music: Harry Potter, The Addams Family; improvisations, solemn tunes, baroque music, Vivaldi, a Poulenc concerto, Pink Floyd, Rolling

Stones, songs: 'Etoile des Neiges', 'Le Vieux Chalet'. My grandmother stands with her eyes closed, listening, arms out in front to balance, like a dancing bear at a fairground. I email my mother: does she realise there's enough here for several whole days of listening? She says he just carried on and on playing. He wanted to send me all of it. He seemed so happy, she says, so happy.

TWO DAYS BEFORE we're due to leave, my grandfather comes home early from work. We eat alone, just the two of us, my grandmother has shut herself in the kitchen to make cakes for the journey. Aromas of honey and frying fill the house. She reappears around eleven with a bag of steaming kkwabaegi, a fifteen-litre bin bag.

'They're the largest ones we have – I know it's not very nice, but I couldn't find anything else to put them in,' she says, setting the bag down at my feet.

'I'll put them with our luggage.'

'No, those are for her. I'm just about to make some for us. Not like that stuff from Family Mart. That child needs to eat fresh food.'

By the time I realise what she means, she's already back in the kitchen. I try one of the doughnuts. It's warm, crunchy.

Henriette still hasn't called back. I'll go and see them tomorrow.

There's an empty space in my room where the boxes were stacked. I feel disoriented. I can't get to sleep. I try lying on the floor, climb back into the bed. I get up and go upstairs to the living room again. There's nothing left for me to do. I move the suitcases around one last time and go out.

I wander aimlessly up and down in front of the house, then turn into the street lined with shops selling leather goods. I walk past the clothing stores, headless mannequins glowing in the windows, lit by the headlights from passing cars. I press on, ready-to-wear shops gradually giving way to ateliers offering bespoke garments, bolts of leather stacked up inside, bulky and heavy.

I retrace my steps, make my way back to Nippori.

Next to McDonald's, the Chinese man winds noodles around his arms, twisting them this way and that, like a marshmallow machine. A sumo wrestler dressed in a tracksuit rides past, pedalling a tiny bike, his topknot waxed and gleaming.

I arrive at the Shiny. My grandfather has unplugged the strings of lights, turned off the neon lighting, the spotlights. With the shopfront darkened like this, I realise how badly lit this end of the street is, with its two meagre streetlights either side of the taxi rank. The main source of light here was the Shiny, attracting all the insects at night.

I bring my face close to the window. With no one to play them, the machines seem pathetic. A single bulb glimmers weakly near the desk, the watchman just discernible in its dim glow. Pachinko balls. For Mieko. I could ask him to give me some, I won't get another chance. Rain starts falling, fine and cold. Autumn rain, with a tang of rust. I realise the summer is over.

I go into McDonald's, order a coffee and sit down by the window. Why so much neon lighting, I wonder, squinting to block out the glare. The coffee has an odd, acidic taste. Rain lashes against the window. An old man comes in carrying a cup on a tray, his mouth twitching. He looks around for somewhere to sit. All the seats are taken. He goes up to the smoking floor. Without quite knowing why, I get up from my seat and follow him upstairs. He's found somewhere to sit at the communal table, a sleeping man next to him on one side, a boy studying on the other. I'd like to tell him he can have my seat but I'd feel stupid, I don't know him. I go back downstairs.

My seat has been taken by a familiar-looking figure. Hair in braids, white trainers, tied in a double knot. I've never seen her without her sandwich boards before. She's shapelier than I imagined. She's wearing a short-sleeved top. Eating a burger and fries.

'Excuse me.'

I lean down in front of her to pick up my tray. She moves back a fraction, still chewing. She shivers, goose-bumps rising in little mounds on her smooth, hairless arms, like worms in wet sand. I stand there, wondering what to say, until it dawns on me that she's utterly unaware

of my existence. She walks over to the bin to throw away the remains of her burger before going back outside onto the street. I watch her as she waits to cross the road, lit by the yellowish glow from the restaurant, the rain falling steadily on her. The light turns to green, she walks briskly across the road and disappears from view.

THAT NIGHT I DREAM of a human figure creeping through the streets, moving like a jackal along narrow alleyways, rummaging through rubbish bins. The city is deserted, it could be New Year's, when everyone has gone to stay with family outside the city. The figure stops in front of every pachinko parlour and peers in through the window, then comes to sit outside the Shiny. The doors are closed, but the person is confident they'll open again soon. Closed for maintenance. The Shiny will be open for business tomorrow. From inside the parlour, the watchman says something to the figure, his mouth opening and closing. I can't make out the words. His coat pockets are filled

with pachinko balls, all the balls from the machines that fill the Shiny.

IN SHINAGAWA, building work is under way. Scaffolding covers the future Promise Hotel, camouflaging the entrance. The lift system has been overhauled, the intercom has gone. No need to buzz anyone in the building, you simply go up. But the lift stops two floors before Henriette and Mieko's. The only way to reach the apartment is by the emergency staircase.

I go up and arrive at the fire door. I knock. No answer. They must not have heard. The door isn't locked, I step inside. I recognise the staircase, the one Mieko and I took to go up to the roof. Another flimsier door opens directly into the kitchen.

No one. A smell of garlic and parmesan hangs in the air. On the table, an opened bottle of royal milk tea. Books lie scattered on the sofa. Everything is bathed in a half-light. I walk along the corridor, darker and narrower now because of the tarpaulin covering the lift.

I go down to the pool.

On the yoga mat, Henriette is lying on her back holding her feet in her hands. She's dressed in a pale pink body-suit that covers her from neck to toe. The instructor's voice murmurs soothingly from a laptop:

'Breathe in, breathe out. The "Happy Baby" pose.'

'It's me,' I call out from the guard rail, feeling quite foolish. 'The door was open.'

Henriette lets go of her feet and raises herself up, slowly unfurling her limbs.

'We never see you any more,' she says.

'I left you a message, I wasn't well. You didn't reply.'

She looks blankly at me.

'Don't worry about it, though,' I add hastily.

'Oh, yes . . . Are you feeling better?'

She smiles.

'Mieko's at school,' she says.

'I thought it started next Monday.'

'Her school organises a camp, before term starts.'

'Camp?'

'A camp,' she says again. 'A week of special activities. Intensive. So the children can all catch up.'

'I didn't know.'

'No reason why you should. You're her teacher, not her mother.'

She stares at me for a moment. Then she steps onto the ramp and goes up the stairs. I follow her up. The bodysuit she's wearing makes her muscles stand out. She holds herself upright – her carriage seems unnaturally stiff for someone who practises yoga. I wonder if she realises how anxious Mieko feels about school. I feel powerless, frustrated.

When we get to the top of the stairs, she doesn't invite me to go through into the living room. She says she doesn't have anything she can offer me to eat.

'I could make a quick trip to the convenience store,' she says. 'If you like.'

'No need,' I reply.

Hovering between us, the image of Henriette, eating crab.

'The building work's started, I see,' I say, nodding towards the tarpaulin across the lift.

'Yes?' she says. 'Was there something else?'

I fumble around in my bag for the CDs.

'They're for Mieko,' I say, handing them to Henriette. 'My father, playing the organ.'

'Does Mieko like organ music?'

'I don't know. But I'd promised her. I wanted to give them to her before I leave for Korea tomorrow.'

'With your grandparents?'

'Yes. We're going by boat.' I describe our itinerary.

'You should have asked me for advice,' she says. 'I know the crossing to Fukuoka by heart. I did it dozens of times with my husband. Before Mieko was born.'

She gives me a kindly look. Almost maternal. Asks me if I've enjoyed my holidays.

'I wish I'd been able to fit more in.'

'I made you work too much.'

'It didn't feel like work,' I confess, feeling slightly guilty. 'Not when I was with Mieko.'

'We teachers spend our holidays preparing our classes, you know.'

'I know,' I say, thinking of Mathieu. 'What will you be teaching this semester?'

She makes a sweeping motion with her hand. 'Jean-Jacques Rousseau,' she says, her speech rapid-fire. 'A first-year course, you'd find it boring, most of the students don't speak much French.'

She hesitates for a moment. Then she asks me if I think Mieko would feel comfortable in Switzerland.

'I can't really say . . .'

'No, I don't suppose you can,' she concurs, speaking more slowly now.

'People get used to things,' I add.

'I worry about her sometimes.'

Silence. The moment passes.

'She wanted me to take her to the zoo,' I say.

'Oh, yes . . . She likes animals.'

Her face takes on a warm glow as she says:

'I had a dog when I was small. At my parents' house, in the country. When they died, he just wasted away. I'd get Mieko one, if I could, but it's difficult, up here at the top of this building. Some day, perhaps. Later.'

She tells me that Mieko finishes at four. Her school isn't far, I can go and meet her and give her the CDs.

'She'll be pleased to see you,' she says ushering me towards the emergency exit.

I ARRIVE EARLY. The pupils are still in the playground, a vast, concrete space. Hundreds of children. I never see any children on the streets. Where have they all come from? A group of boys are kicking a ball around, the girls huddled in groups around the benches. A hubbub of voices, the sounds all dampened on this side of the fence, even the thud of the ball as it bounces. It takes me a while to spot Mieko among the children.

She's on her own, drinking royal milk tea, circling the playground. Occasionally, she stops to peer at something, a detail, a rock perhaps or a crack in the wall. Green cap, fringed skirt. The school uniform makes

her look thinner. It's been ten days since we last met up. She's not expecting me. It occurs to me that she might not recognise me, I should have worn something conspicuous. Such as? I stand close to the gates, in front of the mothers waiting to pick up their children.

The bell rings. The children come out two at a time. To my relief Mieko walks over to me. She takes my hand, apparently not at all surprised to see me.

'So, how's the new class?'

She pulls a long face. The class isn't too bad, the atmosphere is a bit odd though. One of her friends killed himself during the summer. The year before, the teacher made him write 'piggy' on his homework instead of his name, because he was fat.

She holds my hand, chattering as we walk. She doesn't ask where I'm taking her.

We take the train to Ueno Station. When she realises we've arrived at the zoo, she does a few skips.

Gingko trees line the walkways. The nuts have ripened early because of the heatwave. Old men are collecting the harvest, using long-arm grabbers to pick up the nuts that have fallen to the ground, dropping them into baskets

they carry on their backs. Looking up, you can see the whale sculpture on the other side of the park, and the Museum of Natural History.

We amble from cage to cage, saving the deer for the end by unspoken agreement. Mieko has let go of my hand. I'm almost afraid to speak. We've reverted to being awkward in each other's company, distant, as we were when we first met. She smells of almonds; it's nice, I say. This is the only shampoo her mother buys now, she replies.

We come to the aviaries. Children throw corn to the pigeons in front of the vulture enclosure. The great bird stands on a leafless tree, its back turned to us, revealing only its legs, the shrivelled neck. Grains of corn land on its head, scatter on the ground beneath it. The vulture doesn't stir. Crows descend and chase away the pigeons, cawing and flinging themselves against the rails as they peck at the corn. Eventually, the vulture shakes out its body and climbs slowly along the branch. When it reaches the top, it stops, its head touching the rails, and stands completely still, its neck twisted at an awkward angle.

Mieko walks over and gazes up at it.

'What are you doing there?' she enquires softly.

'You see,' I say, 'this is why I don't like zoos. Because of the cages.'

She turns to face me.

'Me neither, I don't like them.'

'I thought you'd enjoy it.'

'So did I.'

'Why did you want to come?'

'You were the one who wanted to. Everything we've done was because you wanted to.'

She stares hard at me. I give in and say, 'You didn't make yourself clear.'

'Calearo,' she repeats. 'Like your name. Calairo,' she says, looking pleased with herself for having made the connection.

The deer are clustered in one enclosure. Mieko climbs up on the guard rail and holds out her hand.

'Do you recognise any from Miyajima?' I ask cheerily. An image of the stuffed deer in the museum flashes through my mind, these creatures' fellow beings, frozen in time, the saccharine tones of the film on evolution playing in an unending loop.

Mieko stretches her arm out further. The deer pay no attention, carry on grazing. I stand behind Mieko to make sure she doesn't see as I take one of my grand-

mother's kkwabaegi out of the bag and wave it in the direction of the deer. One of them sniffs the air listlessly, comes closer. Stops. Takes another step towards us. Mieko trembles.

'Onni, look . . .'

In her excitement, she turns to face me. I don't have time to hide the doughnut. I try to look as if I'm eating it, but she's not fooled. She turns back towards the enclosure; the deer has moved away.

I place a hand on her back.

'You know, the deer in the zoo, they're not very healthy.'

'I'm the one who's got something wrong with me,' she says, detaching herself from my grasp.

I can't help laughing. She looks crestfallen.

'It's all lumpy, that doughnut,' she says.

I give it to her, show her my bag and say my grandmother has made lots of them for her. She sniffs it, says it smells good but doesn't bite into it.

'I have some CDs of my father playing the organ too. I wanted to bring you some pachinko balls. But they're heavy. Mucky. It's not worth it, take my word. I swear. They're not like you think they are. They're not toys.'

She didn't think they were toys, she says, her voice barely audible. But it doesn't matter.

'I'm leaving tomorrow, you know. I'm taking my grandparents to Korea.'

'Forever?' she asks.

I shake my head. She doesn't respond.

'What's the matter?' I ask, my voice sounding unnaturally squeaky.

She bites into a doughnut. Then she smiles at me. Nothing. She's happy. She hopes we'll like it, all the way over there.

IN THE TRAIN on the way back, we stand, amid the crush of rush-hour commuters, our bags wedged between our calves. Mieko is too short to hold the ceiling straps. I hang on to her by her jacket.

'I thought of something,' she says after a few minutes. 'We ought to shed our skins, like animals. The older we got, the more transparent our skin would become. In the end you'd be able to see all our insides through it. Veins, bones, feelings, everything. Our skin would be a mirror too, people would be able to see themselves in it. Eventually we'd become completely transparent, and when that happened, we'd give our last breath to our child.'

'Our child?'

'Yes. The one that goes on living after.'

'After us?' I say, correcting her. 'Is that what you mean?'

She doesn't respond.

'What if you don't have any children? Or if you don't want to have any?'

She thinks for a while.

'You still have to die,' she says.

We sway against each other as the train swings from side to side.

Neither of us speaks for the next three stops.

'Would it be painful?' I ask.

'No. We'd just get lighter and lighter, that's all.'

At Shinagawa station I walk as far as the exit with her. I give her the CDs and the kkwabaegi by the main entrance. The straps of her backpack are flapping about loosely. She stands still while I tighten them for her. I tap her lightly on the shoulder when I've finished.

'We haven't spoken much French . . .'

'No.'

'You can tell your mother if you want.'

'Tell her what?'

'That she's a much better teacher than I am.'

Mieko gives me a funny look. I laugh, my hand still on her shoulder. She giggles. And then we both start laughing hysterically. She wraps her arms round my waist. People give us a wide berth as they walk by. We laugh until we're almost crying.

'You're like a mum to me,' Mieko says, burrowing her head into my stomach.

She gives me a squeeze, then relaxes her grip. Before I have time to respond, she disappears into the crowd.

MY GRANDMOTHER SITS cross-legged on the seat, her hands pressed to the window. She's no bigger than a child. Neither of them has said a word since we left the house.

We change trains at Hiroshima and take the Japan Railways Sanyo line to Miyajimaguchi, where we pick up the ferry to the island of Miyajima.

Our guesthouse looks out over the sea. The room we're in has been recently refurbished. It smells of bamboo.

From the balcony you can see the ferry and the torii, the great red gate standing in the water. It looks more orange than red in this late afternoon light. The photos of it used in the tourist brochures have probably been retouched.

My grandmother unrolls the futons, covers them with a sheet. I'm exhausted, I want to burrow under the sheet and not stir until morning, but if my grandmother goes to sleep now, she'll wake us all up in the middle of the night. I suggest we go for a walk.

Low tide. Ducks paddle in the shallow water. The red boardwalks of Itsukushima Shrine flow out over the sand like a carpet of blood. At the entrance, visitors are funnelled past an orange box. A white plastic horse's head sticks out above the box, empty-eyed. I stand on my tiptoes, trying to see the rest of its body, but all I can make out in the gloom is a manger filled with coins.

We stroll along the beach for a while before heading back to the village. On the square where the market stalls are,

a gaggle of elderly people are trying to organise them-
selves for a group photo. There must be about thirty of
them, all dressed in hiking gear and carrying knapsacks,
shouting and gesticulating as they shuffle into place,
smallest at the front, tallest at the back. The photogra-
pher sees my grandparents, grabs them by the collar and
steers them towards the group.

'They're not with us, they're not with us!' the hikers
cry indignantly.

My grandparents have instinctively obeyed the photo-
grapher's instructions. They're pushed from one member
of the group to another before being expelled through a
gap between two women in blue baseball caps. 'Tsk, tsk!'
the women hiss.

They scurry away from the group, clutching each
other by the shoulder, nervously peering around in
search of me. I usher them away and guide them towards
an aquarium open to the public for a modest fee.

A voice booms from a loudspeaker within the enclo-
sure: 'Attention all visitors. The seal show is about to
begin!'

We sit down on a bench, eat some doughnuts. A
family of deer approaches us. My grandmother feeds
them her doughnut, holding it out with the wrapping

still attached. They jostle for scraps. I tell her you're not supposed to feed wild animals. She retorts that the doughnuts have gone soft, the deer are hungry. My grandfather gestures to me to leave her alone. She carries on feeding the deer while we look on. Other deer come right up to her, each one taking its turn. She tickles their heads as they feed, thrilled.

We go to an eel restaurant for dinner. Posters of sumo stars on the walls. The grand championship has just finished in Tokyo. The scores are displayed on a board. An old man sits off to the side, alone, drinking his soup. A young American couple, just finishing their meal, stand up and glance over at us as they leave. I order eel with rice, sweet flesh that melts in the mouth.

Later, my grandfather has a smoke on our bedroom balcony and I go out to join him. Behind the torii gate, the last rays of the setting sun glimmer on the water, Hiroshima in shadow in the distance. We watch the ferry bringing back the commuters and the last tourists of the day from the other shore.

'You don't have to do this,' he says to me in Japanese.

I take a good look at him. His lined forehead, his movements weighed down by an immense fatigue, his breathing laboured.

This trip might not work out the way I imagine, he says. I'd like to tell him that I'm not imagining anything, but he continues, punctuating his speech with lengthy pauses.

'When Korea was divided, we were still nationals of a unified Korea. It was called Choson. At separation, the Japanese government gave us permission to keep our Korean identity, but we had to choose between North and South. Many people chose the North, because of their family or because they considered the North more in line with our country's traditions. There was no way of knowing how things would turn out. Your grandmother and I chose the South because we were from Seoul. That was the only reason. We knew nothing about any of the rest of it. Political questions meant nothing to us, the Cold War, Russia, the United States. Koreans who live in Japan have never known North and South Korea. We are all people of Choson. People from a country that no longer exists.'

He pauses. Then adds, 'We do still have our language.'

I'm sorry I've forgotten how to speak it, I say in Japanese. If my mother hadn't left to go abroad, if I'd

been born somewhere other than Switzerland ... He stops me. Asks me not to criticise my mother's choices. He and my grandmother fled Korea so she could be born in a country free of war. He has always hated the Shiny. My mother grew up. She wanted to leave and she left. Their only desire was for her to live her life according to her own choices.

He looks at me affectionately. And now, here I am, he says. I feel myself blushing.

We stand there, side by side, for a while. My grandfather lights up another cigarette. Smoke coils around his face, the wind catching the halo as soon as it forms. A few moments later, I say I'm going out again, to stretch my legs a bit.

I walk along the main street. The air feels chill, damp. I pull my jacket tighter. Grilles are drawn across the market stalls. My mouth feels dry. I stop at a vending machine, weigh up the options. Coffee with milk, lemon tea, corn soup, empty compartments. I lick my lips to moisten them. Beyond the walls of the aquarium the loudspeaker still blares.

'Attention all visitors! The seal show is about to begin!'

I imagine groups of children huddled on the terraces, left behind by their parents after the last ferry has gone.

The mountain rises beyond the village. In the shadows, a large building in the traditional style, curved roof, a hotel perhaps. Gravel gives way to greenery underfoot. The ferns make a rustling sound as I weave my way among them. Rusting copper containers lie on the earth. A pond, mosquitoes. I come to a gate, push it open and walk on, all the way to the building.

Up close it seems much smaller, the façade crumbling. I use the torch on my phone to shine a light through one of the windows. A counter littered with debris, a dial phone. Shattered windowpanes, rooms emptied out. A kitchen. On the table, biscuit wrappers, a jar of pickles, greenish, floating like embryos.

A haikyo. A building abandoned by the owners, left to fall into ruin, a cheaper option than demolition. Japan is littered with them.

I back out. As I close the gate, I feel something wet brushing against my hand. I turn round with a start.

A deer. Staring at me, warily, keeping its distance. Dirty thing, I mutter, my heart beating wildly, reassured nevertheless to know that I'm not alone.

I go back to the village, forcing myself to walk slowly. Walking any faster would mean admitting that I'm scared. The deer follows me, stopping occasionally then trotting a little faster to catch up.

The aquarium has fallen silent. At the entrance, a woman is busy with a brush and a bucket. She bows low, disappears inside through a service entrance.

A MONOTONOUS LANDSCAPE of plains that dissolve on the horizon. Houses dotted about, lightweight boxes, scraps of wood, scattered like pawns across a chess board. Forests of trees bending in the wind. Inside the train, the air is still. The Shinkansen heads due south, the sky darkening as we advance.

At the station in Hakata, we take the bus to the port of Fukuoka. The bus carries us through the business district, a residential area, wasteland. Cranes loom in the mist, containers stacked up behind them. We arrive at the

embarkation quay. A large building, a wedding venue by the looks of it, with a restaurant, a ballroom and a portrait stage. My grandparents say they'll wait here while I go and check us in. I know it's merely a delaying tactic, a way to avoid meeting the other passengers. When I come back, I find them in the restaurant. My grandmother has ordered soup, my grandfather a squid salad.

I watch them as they eat.

My grandmother swallows her food rapidly. My grandfather too, their movements in sync as they nourish their ageing bodies. How alike they are, I reflect. They've lived alongside each other for so long, their features seem to merge into one another.

The boarding area is crowded, the seats in the waiting room all occupied. Koreans everywhere: teenagers; a middle-aged couple; a baseball team, talking loudly, laughing. A boy spits. I can feel my grandmother beside me, the pressure of her hand in mine, her nails pressed to my palm. Damp. I squeeze her hand back. Outside, mist obscures the horizon. The ships in the port are scarcely visible, the containers like splashes of watercolour.

'My nails have turned black. Look.'

My grandmother waves her hand in my face. I push it away gently.

'That happens, you scratched the deer.'

My grandfather rubs her back to warm her up. He keeps standing up to check the locks on our suitcases, he's afraid he'll forget the code. The stewardess's voice rings out, in Japanese, boarding will commence soon. The baseball players come back from the food stand with bottles of water, biscuits. My grandmother fusses. Maybe we should do the same, buy water, biscuits. I agree, without thinking. The stewardess is getting ready to open the access to the walkway.

We stand motionless, all three of us, in the waiting area, watching her. My grandmother tightens her grip on me.

'You're hurting me.'

'I want to go home,' she replies.

'That's where we're going.'

'This is the wrong way.'

'No, it's not,' I say. 'We're going to Korea.'

She looks all round her again.

'I want to go home.'

I don't know what to do. I make up an excuse about forgetting something in the restaurant and go back outside, onto the quayside.

I call Mathieu. It's four in the morning there. To my relief, he picks up. He's back in Geneva, he'd left his phone on in case I needed him. I tell him they've changed their minds, they don't want to go. Mathieu says nothing at first. Then, quite simply, he asks if I want him to come over.

'No, I'll come back to Switzerland. I can't do any more here.'

'Yes, you can,' he says. 'You should go. You're the one who needs to go.'

'If they don't go back to Korea now, they never will. I can't leave them by themselves, not here. What am I supposed to do? I can't leave them on their own.'

Panic makes me talk faster and faster. Mathieu is unruffled, his voice calm.

'They've been living there for fifty years. They'd already been there for twenty years when you were born.'

I cram my phone to my chest. The mist has turned to rain, falling steadily on the concrete. Crane drivers emerge from their cockpits and scurry into the warehouses. I raise the phone to my lips. Tell Mathieu that I'm going to Korea, I don't know how long for. He may have to wait for me. He'll wait, he replies.

When I get back to the waiting area, all the passengers have gone. Only my grandparents remain; my grandmother is gesticulating, trying to tell the stewardess I'm on my way back. The stewardess catches sight of me, smiles and asks for our tickets. We're late, she says, it's time to leave. I feel my grandmother shoving me from behind.

'Okay, okay, go, go!' she chirps.

I step onto the gangplank, clutch the handrail. The walkway feels slippery underfoot. A voice booms from the loudspeaker: welcome aboard, security instructions in Japanese first, then in Korean. It's hard to see the inside of the ship, there's too much condensation. Passengers trace shapes on the portholes with their fingertips.

Halfway along, I look back. My grandparents are rooted to the spot. The stewardess has closed the barrier. I freeze. My grandfather has his arm round my grandmother. She waves at me to say goodbye. I make a move in their direction, but I can see them mouthing: 'Go, go.'

I raise my hand high in the air, wave to them as I step onto the boat. The loudspeakers have fallen silent.

All that lingers is an echo. A clamour of languages merging gradually to become one.